"Travis? Have You Seen A Little Boy With Dark Hair?"

"You mean Brandon? He's right here—asleep. I don't know very much about kids, Alexis, but he feels awfully hot to me."

Alexis stepped closer to the porch swing, knelt at their feet and placed her hand on the little boy's forehead. "You're right. He does feel warm. I hope he's not coming down with something. Would you mind carrying him home? He only lives next door."

Travis welcomed the activity. The prospect of carrying a fifty-pound kid a few hundred feet was a lot less disturbing than having Alexis kneeling at his feet. He picked up the sleeping boy, who fit easily in his arms. This was getting out of hand. First Alexis had gotten under his skin, then the kid.

Travis had a job to do—a score to settle with a killer. It was ridiculous to be standing in the damn moonlight wondering what it would be like if he and Alexis were a real family....

Dear Reader,

I know you can't wait to get your hands on September's Silhouette Desire books! First, because September has the latest installment in Diana Palmer's MOST WANTED series—*The Case of the Missing Secretary.* And don't worry if you missed earlier books in the series; each story stands on its own.

Next, because September has Annette Broadrick, and the start of her new series, the SONS OF TEXAS. This month we have *Love Texas Style!* Look for *Courtship Texas Style!* in October and *Marriage Texas Style!* in November.

And, of course, there's this month's thrilling, sexy, wonderful *Man of the Month, Navarrone,* by Helen R. Myers. And September is completed with fabulous stories by Laura Leone, Jean Barrett and a talented newcomer I know you'll love, Mary Maxwell.

Don't miss any of these. I couldn't begin to pick a favorite—they're all so terrific—and I'll bet you couldn't, either.

All the best,

Lucia Macro
Senior Editor

MARY MAXWELL
DOUBLECROSS

SILHOUETTE *Desire*

Published by Silhouette Books New York

America's Publisher of Contemporary Romance

SILHOUETTE BOOKS
300 East 42nd St., New York, N.Y. 10017

DOUBLECROSS

ISBN: 0-373-05735-0

First Silhouette Books printing September 1992

MARY MAXWELL

is married to a terrific guy and lives with him and their two daughters and three cats in a suburban community outside of Seattle, Washington. A voracious reader, she is a fan of romance novels because she feels they are a positive voice in a sometimes negative world. Everyone, she believes, sometimes needs a reminder that love makes all things possible—and that dreams do come true.

To Max and Tim and all the other wonderful people
who helped make this book a reality—*thank you.*

One

"**W**ell, hell." Slouched against a wall outside the entrance to the shopping center, Travis Cross's intense curse was distinctly at odds with his negligent posture. No one observing the tall, jeans-clad figure, hands jammed into his pockets, broad shoulders angled against the building, would guess at the sheer fury swirling through him.

His dark blue eyes narrowed behind his aviator-style sunglasses as he looked once more across the nearly deserted parking lot to where his rental car was parked. The nondescript sedan stood in forlorn isolation, listing noticeably to the left.

His jaw clenched. This was not the time for a flat tire—not when they were on to him. Hell. They were *after* him.

He swore again, a long, lethal string of words issued under his breath, shoving a hand impatiently through his dark, shaggy hair. He'd told MacGregor he was too damned old for this. Too old for the intrigue, too weary for the machinations.

The bureau chief had simply smiled, coaxing him from a five-month leave by the simple expedient of refusing to take no for an answer. *I need you, Cross.... Nobody else will do, Cross.... Come on, Cross—this could be our last shot to get LeClair. Or do you want Joel's murderer to get off scot free?*

It was the last part that had gotten Travis, just as MacGregor had known it would. That, and the fact that it fit right in with his own plans, since, with or without the Department's sanction, he planned to get the man responsible for the death of his best friend.

Only this wasn't exactly what he'd envisioned when he'd been sitting in the stark kitchen of his isolated Connecticut farm, imagining the downfall of Joel's murderer.

But then, who would have dreamed that in forty-eight hours he'd find himself transported to a suburban Seattle shopping center, a loaded Sig P238 nestled against the small of his back, three and a half million dollars worth of stolen diamonds strapped to his ankle, and a getaway car with a flat?

Well, hell.

Holding the sleek black Ferrari steady, Alexis Wright swatted ineffectively at the sea of helium-inflated balloons undulating around her head and downshifted into second. She glanced at the dashboard clock. Darn! It was already four-fifty—she was running late!

With a deft flick of her wrist, she roared into the parking lot of her favorite one-stop shopping emporium and angled into a parking slot next to the back entrance. Despite the need for haste, she paused a minute to appreciate the steady rumble of the sports car's powerful engine. An old Supremes song boomed from the tape deck and she couldn't contain a grin. One way or another, she was going to make this April Fool's Day party the best one ever for the kids.

Clicking off the engine, she slipped from the car and dashed into the store. In less than ten minutes she was back in the car, two gallons of chocolate-ripple ice cream tucked into the space behind the passenger seat.

Smiling with satisfaction at how quickly this final errand had gone, she fastened her seat belt, slid in the clutch, inserted the key in the ignition and twisted.

Several things happened at once.

The engine roared. The stereo blared. And a total stranger wrenched open the passenger door, hurled himself into the low-slung vehicle and shouted, "Drive!"

Alex stared at him in amazement, shocked by his abrupt appearance, and said the first thing that came to mind. "No."

He swiveled to face her. "What do you mean—*no?*" His expression was almost comically incredulous.

"I said *no*," she repeated, leaning forward to turn down the stereo. Quickly sensing that her unruffled reaction had a far better chance of disarming him than hysteria, she settled back against the ebony leather upholstery, folded her arms across her chest and turned slightly to get a better look at him. "This isn't Miami, you're definitely too tall to be Don Johnson, and I'm already running behind schedule. Besides, I never pick up strangers—it isn't safe." Automatically, she noted his thick dark hair, the broad shoulders filling the expensive leather jacket and his long muscular legs, which disappeared into custom cowboy boots. From the tips of that shining hair to the toes of his impressive physique, he was one gorgeous man.

She'd be able to pick him out of a lineup anywhere.

He muttered something that had nothing to do with either safety or strangers, something she was certain was anatomically impossible, besides. Reaching inside his coat, he yanked out a leather card case, flipped it open and impatiently shoved it in her face. "Travis Cross. SDSS," he gritted out. "Now drive, damn it."

Taking the case from his hand, Alex studied the silver badge pinned to the battered leather and the photo ID below it. "Hmm. State Department Special Services? Never heard of it." Despite her flip words, the coil of fear that had been twisting her insides from the instant he'd jumped into her car began to unwind at this evidence that he was one of the good guys. Her gaze shifted from the photo in her hand to her unwanted passenger's face. "Take off your sunglasses," she instructed.

He whipped them off, glaring at her out of flame-blue eyes. "Okay? Satisfied it's me?"

Relaxing even more at his total—but strictly nonviolent—exasperation with her, the slightest of smiles curved her generous mouth. "Well," she conceded, stifling her relieved amusement, "it's you all right."

"Great! Now that that's settled, can we get the hell out of here? Please?" he added sarcastically.

Her gaze shifted beyond him as two tough-looking men came racing out of the store, clearly agitated about something. Although dressed in well-cut suits, they looked more like wrestlers than businessmen. Intrigued both by their odd appearance, as well as their behavior as they skidded to a halt and looked wildly around, she remarked idly, "Oh, sorry, but the answer's still no. Your ID's expired."

"Give me that!" he snarled, snatching the card case out of her hand to examine it in the fading early-evening light.

Still watching the tableau unfolding on the sidewalk, she experienced her first twinge of uneasiness when one of the men spotted her car. He stared at it, an arrested expression coming over his heavy features before he said something that caused the other man to jerk around and stare, too. The pair held a hurried conference, then started toward the Ferrari. One of them slipped his hand inside his suit coat. When the hand emerged, it was clutching a gun.

"Hmm." Alex believed in following her instincts, and the same instinct that had assured her Travis Cross wouldn't harm her was now telling her something very different about the approaching men. "Are you being chased, by chance?" she inquired.

Still staring in irritated disbelief at his expired identification, it was a few seconds before the question penetrated Travis's consciousness. When it did, his head jerked up and he glanced out the window. "Holy hell."

"Friends of yours?"

She could see his body coil with tension. "No." He took a swift look around, and an expression of wonder flitted across his features when he belatedly noticed the two-dozen balloons bobbing on the end of their strings in the abbreviated back seat.

After a swift look at Alex, which stated clearly that he seriously doubted her sanity, he gave the rapidly approaching men one last glance through the Ferrari's tinted windows. Then his lips tightened and he appeared to reach a decision.

With the precise grace of someone who has made a particular move countless times before, he reached around and pulled a gun from his waistband. Hand rock steady, eyes totally calm, he took aim. At Alex.

She stiffened, staring in surprise.

"Lady, I am done debating with you." Every word was very clearly enunciated, the effort he was making to control himself obvious in each bitten-off syllable. "Move the damn car. Now!"

For an interminable second, Alex stared at him, considering. Common sense told her unequivocally that Travis Cross, heartthrob of the State Department, was definitely not going to shoot her. Still, the thugs on the sidewalk were almost upon them; she was willing to concede the wisdom of a quick departure.

She released the parking brake and shifted into reverse, effortlessly guiding the Ferrari as it skated smoothly backward. The thugs hurried past without giving them so much as a second glance. In gratified disbelief, Alex watched them zero in instead on a white sedan with a dark-haired male driver who was parked farther down the lot.

"Good," Travis said. When Alex shot him a glance, he motioned curtly with the hand still holding the gun, a sardonic tilt to his chiseled mouth. "Well? *Drive.* Or don't you see the wisdom in being long gone before they recognize their mistake?"

It was about time, Alex decided as she went from reverse to first in a blur of motion, to teach Mr. Travis Cross—SOS or DDS or whatever!—a much-needed lesson. He might be a hunk, even a licensed *government* hunk, but that didn't give him the right to go around threatening private citizens with a gun.

Nor, she concluded, her eyes narrowing briefly on the cynical twist to his sensual lips, would he suffer from a brief demonstration of the pitfalls of overconfidence. "It's always been my opinion," she began reasonably enough, "that if you really want to try and frighten someone with a gun, you should always be sure to release the safety. Otherwise—" she accelerated, popping the gearshift into second "—you run the risk that your intended victim might know something about firearms and decide to retaliate." With a twist of the steering wheel she whipped out of the parking lot, throwing Travis into the door as she swerved onto the heavily traveled two-lane road with the speed of a cork launched from a champagne bottle.

Accelerating relentlessly, she deftly went from second to third to fourth and, as the sleek black car picked up speed, blithely began to weave in and out of traffic. After nonchalantly negotiating a series of near misses, she glanced at Travis. He looked slightly pale.

A quick survey of the traffic signal as they approached a major intersection told its own story as the light changed from green to yellow. Bottom lip caught between her straight white teeth, eyes narrowed in concentration, Alex pressed the accelerator to the floor and shot between two vans, flying across the bisecting thoroughfare just as the light turned red. "Jeez! Watch out, lady!" her passenger yelped as they were nearly sideswiped by a Metro bus.

She didn't turn a hair. "It's also rarely wise—" she pretended not to hear his strangled gasp as she swung briefly into the oncoming lane to get around a slower vehicle "—to try and intimidate someone who's just as lethally armed as you are."

He mumbled something she couldn't quite make out in response to this particular observation. She couldn't stop the dimple that appeared briefly in one smooth cheek as she reflected that was probably for the best. She had a sneaking suspicion he'd said something obscene.

Sweeping onto the northbound freeway with the velocity of an arrow shot from a bow, she turned her head and favored him with a demure smile. "Now, I don't know about you," she said, reaching out and gently pushing the gun barrel in a direction away from herself, "but I personally feel that a Ferrari doing—" she glanced at the speedometer "—eighty miles an hour during rush hour," she continued, one hand on the wheel, the other waving casually at the congested traffic all around them, "qualifies as at least *po-*

tentially lethal.'' She shot him a questioning glance as she zoomed onto the left shoulder in order to pass a car doing a mere sixty-five. "What do you think?"

"Damn it to hell!" Travis hastily shoved the gun in his waistband and reached for his seat belt, fastening it with a desperate click. "I think you should watch the damn road—and slow down!"

She sent him a quelling look. "You really ought to do something about your language," she chided, unperturbed by his outburst. Shooting across four lanes of traffic, she added knowingly, "Swearing can get to be a hard habit to break, Mr. Cross." With a flick of her wrist, she skillfully wedged the car into a minuscule opening in the far right-hand lane and zoomed down an off ramp, sedately braking at the four-way stop at the end of it before turning right.

Travis stared at her, incredulous at the discrepancy between her serene manner and her kamikaze highway tactics. Bemused, he watched as once more, she went through the gears with effortless mastery. While the man in him might note—and appreciate—her elegant bone structure, soft creamy skin and the tawny golden braid thick as his wrist that hung to her waist, the agent in him—drilled in survival—was screaming, *Mayday! Mayday! Eject! Eject!* She might look like an angel, but she drove like a bat out of hell!

"Look—" To his chagrin, his voice sounded hoarse. "What do you do for a living, crash-test Volvos?"

She gave him an innocent smile. "Nothing that exotic. I'm a professor at the university. I teach languages."

"Yeah, right." He didn't believe it for a minute. If she was a teacher, he was a soprano for the Met. Glancing out the window, he realized it was nearly dark, and that they were now traveling—at the speed of sound—due east on a winding two-lane country road bracketed by scrub alder and evergreen trees. "Just drop me at the nearest store or gas station."

She glanced at him in surprise, then at the clock. For the first time since they'd met, she appeared just the slightest bit distressed. "Um, are you in a hurry? I mean, is your business urgent?"

Travis couldn't believe it. Was she kidding? Blinking, he peered at her, took in her earnest expression, then rubbed his eyes in disbelief. He took a few deep breaths, trying to get a handle on his escalating sense of being caught in some weird dream.

It didn't help. "Are you out of your mind?" he demanded, twisting in his seat to glare at her. She might not know about the diamonds, but she sure as hell had seen his pursuers! "Didn't you see those two guys? One of them had a gun! What do you think he was doing—carrying it just for effect? Of *course* I'm in a hurry! What lunatic asylum did you escape from, huh, lady?"

"Hey. Calm down." To his amazement, she reached over in a gentle, placating gesture and laid her hand on his thigh. "Relax. There's nothing to get so upset about." She gave him a reassuring little pat, taking her eyes from the road long enough to give him a calm, pacifying look with her big brown eyes. "Of course I saw them. And I realize why one of them had a gun," she admonished in that same soothing tone. It was the kind of tone parents use on hysterical children. Or dog owners on recalcitrant pets!

"But—" with another of those casual gestures he found so paralyzing, she took her other hand from the wheel and waved it in a sweeping arc "—do you see him now? Of course not. Look around. We're in the boonies. We haven't seen another car in at least—"

"Would-you-please-keep-one-hand-on-the-damn-steering-wheel!" he gritted out between clenched teeth.

She shot him an amused look but indulgently took hold of the wheel again with her left hand. "Okay? Better?" She gave his thigh a gentle squeeze with her right hand. "Now, where was I? Oh, yes." Again she glanced at the clock. "I was trying to point out that the immediate risk, at least, is over. Because," she said, the faintest note of apology creeping into her tone, "in roughly forty minutes I have fourteen children ranging in age from six to eleven arriving at my house for a party, and—" she took a deep breath as if to fortify herself against his anticipated reaction to her next statement "—I can't spare the time to run you to the nearest gas station. It's back by the off ramp. You really should have said something sooner."

Travis told himself to stay calm, reminding himself there was nothing to be gained by getting upset. She couldn't possibly be serious, could she? "You're kidding, right? I mean, I believe you about the party—that, at least, explains the weird balloons. But not the other. There's gotta be something out here!" His voice was taking on a desperate tone; once more he cautioned himself to calm down. "I mean," he said more reasonably, "this is hardly the Aussie outback or the wilds of Africa. It's no big deal—it doesn't have to be anything fancy. Just a phone booth will do—okay?"

"All you need is someplace with a phone?"

"That's all."

"Really?"

"That's it."

"If that's all you need, no problem."

Travis sighed with relief.

"You can call from my house." Downshifting, Alex swung the car to the left and they swept past a sign proclaiming the entrance to Cedar Creek Estates.

"No, I bloody well won't!" he roared, all his hard-won cool evaporating in an instant. "Don't you get it? I need to get back to Seattle! And in order to do that, I need a ride! Now, I can accomplish that two ways, lady—I can either call a cab or I can contact my backup. The problem with doing either of those is that I'm going to have to reveal my location in order to be picked up, and if anybody is monitoring those dispatches, that's going to lead them right to you and your eleven fourteen-year-olds or four five-year-olds or whatever the hell it is, and I don't think you want that!"

"It's fourteen kids of various ages, and no, I don't," Alex remonstrated mildly, turning the car into the semicircular driveway that ran around the back of the big, rambling old farmhouse she called home. Parking in the carport, which was attached to the house by a graceful covered walkway, she turned off the engine, unsnapped her seat belt and calmly swiveled to face her irate passenger.

"But, Mr. SDS or Bar-S or *whoever* it is you work for, neither do I have any intention of ruining my party just because some government spy-boy has a hot date downtown.

"As I see it," she continued, "you have two choices. Either you can stay here and relax for a little while and after the party I'll be happy to take you anywhere you want to go, no questions asked, or, you can start walking. It's about twelve miles back to the freeway and you look like you're in pretty good shape. It shouldn't take you more than two hours. The choice—" she opened her car door "—is yours. Oh, and by the way," she said over her shoulder, "quit calling me 'lady.' My name is Alex—Alexis Wright. Now, if you'll excuse me, I've got things to do." She levered herself gracefully out of the car.

Furious, Travis followed suit, slamming the door behind him with a resounding bang. His eyes glittered dangerously as he confronted her. "You know, *lady,* you are seriously getting on my nerves." Bracing his hands against the roof of the low-slung car, he regarded her across its gleaming surface. "Let's get a few things straight. First, I'll call you *lady* if I damn well want to. Second, I am not in *pretty good shape*," he mimicked her earlier words. "I happen to be in *great* shape. And, third," he said, surreptitiously eyeing the car keys dangling in her hand, reflecting that he'd always wanted to drive a Ferrari, "it occurs to me that I have one more option."

"Really?" she inquired politely.

"Yeah, really."

"I wouldn't bet on it," she said sweetly. As if she could read his mind, she smiled guilelessly at him in the same instant that she brought her arm back and threw the keys with all her might.

"Damn it!" Travis jumped out of the way as the keys whizzed by his ear with a speed Joe Namath would have envied. "What the hell are you trying to do!" he roared, twisting around just in time to see them disappear in the general direction of a patch of ground that bore a striking resemblance to the Amazon jungle. "Decapitate me?"

Alex smiled serenely. "Hardly. Assuming Option Number Three was stealing my car, I suggest you reconsider. I highly recommend you don't attempt to hot-wire it," she advised, correctly interpreting the newest gleam in his eye. "I bought it with an optional antitheft device guaranteed to shock the socks off anybody who tampers with the ignition.

"However, if you're determined," she said, gesturing eloquently at the tangled growth behind him, "be my guest. It shouldn't take you more than, say—" she pursed her lips speculatively "—three hours to find the keys. As I said, it's your choice, Mr. Cross."

Reaching back into the car, she grabbed a fistful of balloon strings, picked up the bag that held the ice cream and marched to the back door, kicking over a rock on the way to scoop up a spare house key from beneath it. Pulling open the screen, she opened the back door and flicked on the porch lights before disappearing inside.

Travis watched as the interior lights bloomed on, revealing a big, old-fashioned, two-story farmhouse with a covered porch that encircled the entire first floor. Here and there he could see painted wicker furniture sporting boldly colored cushions grouped cozily at strategic points along the broad veranda. In the far corner, an enormous potted fern hung by a chain from the roof, casting tentaclelike shadows across the floor.

He liked the place on sight. Painted a spanking white, it was a comfortable-looking house that had quite obviously been lavished with generous amounts of love and care over the years. It was homey. And Travis had never felt at home anywhere in his life, certainly not in any of the swank boarding schools his mother had shunted him off to, or any of the mansions he'd visited briefly during holidays spent with her and her constantly changing cast of husbands.

He debated what to do.

On a good day, he could do a nine-minute mile without straining himself, but that was when he was wearing running shoes. Staring down at his ornately tooled cowboy boots, he conceded they were hardly made for jogging.

And he didn't doubt Alex Wright was telling him the truth about the theft preventer on her car. The Ferrari would be a prime candidate for auto thieves; she'd be a fool to drive around in it without such a safeguard.

He supposed he could look for the damn keys. Hell, he might even find them. Eventually. Although—he turned and surveyed the wilderness she called her backyard—he doubted it would take three hours. More like three years. And did he want to run the risk of being attacked and possibly eaten by whatever inhabited all that shrubbery? With his luck, Alexis Wright probably bred wolves or rattlesnakes or something else equally as dangerous just for fun.

She was the damnedest woman he'd ever met.

As if on cue, the screen door opened and she marched back down the walkway. For just a minute he allowed himself the luxury of admiring the lithe, easy way she moved, her braid swinging like a pendulum, as she walked past him and retrieved something big and rectangular and flat from the back of the car.

Straightening, she turned and faced him. "I'm sorry I lost my temper," she said, in that soft calm voice he was beginning to realize was very much a part of her. "And I want you to know my offer still stands. I'll be happy to take you into Seattle just as soon as the party's over. I'm sorry if you're not very happy with the way this turned out, but then," she pointed out reasonably, "you jumped in my car. I didn't invite you." She shrugged. "Regardless, it's pointless to stand around out in the yard all night, so why don't you come on in? It's dark out here." She shivered. "And cold."

Travis stared at her, amazed as much by her apology— after all, he *had* hijacked her and not the other way around—as by the revelation that she'd lost her temper.

When? Was that what that patient little speech earlier about his choices had been? A demonstration of her temper? Hell. If that was a temper tantrum, what did she do to let people know when she was a little miffed? Carry a sign? Put a notice in the newspaper?

"Well. Come in if you want to," she said softly. Leaving him to make his own decision, she walked away and disappeared back into the house.

Travis stood for another minute. She really was something, he decided. There was a serenity about her that was unlike anything he'd ever encountered. And that attracted him unlike anything else could have.

He scowled. If there was one thing he knew, it was that attractions were synonymous with trouble. Oh, not the "hi there, I like your body, let's go to bed" kind of mutual appeal; that was lust, biological and understandable and mutually pleasurable between consenting, realistic adults. No, what you had to watch out for was the "it's love and we're going to live happily ever after" kind of delusion that so much of humanity was, unfortunately, prone to believe in.

Travis, having watched his mother destroy herself trying to fulfill that particular fantasy, had never been the least bit tempted by it himself. At least, not until now. Not until Alexis Wright who, with her calm competency, satin-smooth skin and welcoming house, was both a walking invitation to sin—and a temptation he didn't care to risk. He had a mission to accomplish—a murder to avenge.

Still, he couldn't stand around out here all night.

Sighing, he moved to the car door, reached in and snagged the last few balloons, then carefully shut the door before starting up the walkway after her.

Well, hell. Why not? After all, the second the party was over, he was out of here.

Two

"**J**ust what in Sam Hill do you mean, you've got the diamonds?"

Travis jerked the phone away from his ear as MacGregor let loose a string of curses strong enough to strip the shine off a no-wax floor. Leaning back against a kitchen counter, he propped one cowboy boot over the other, his dark blue eyes taking in his surroundings as he waited for the bureau chief to wind down.

An enormous country kitchen ran across the back of Alex's house. It was a cheerful room, with burnished oak floors and walls done in white with bright splashes of blue. A variety of plants abounded, from a cascade of green over one side of a state-of-the-art, built-in refrigerator to a small African violet covered with delicate lavender flowers sitting in a dish next to the big double sink. A round oak table graced one corner, next to a bank of windows that faced east to catch the morning sun. Grouped around it were four high-tech club chairs, plushly padded and built for comfort.

From force of habit, the first thing Travis had done when he entered the house was make a fast but complete tour of the premises; it was probably unnecessary, but experience had taught him it was just such attention to little details that could mean the difference between success and failure—or life and death. His quick inspection had shown him that the kitchen was pretty representative of the rest of the house. Old and new, traditional and modern, antique and high tech, all were blended throughout to make a home that was exceptionally comfortable, quite beautiful and very restful.

Except for Alex's bedroom, Travis amended. Comfortable and attractive—yes. But restful? *No.* It was like something out of a harem movie. Just picturing it made his blood pressure rise. The wood floor was covered by an ankle-deep Persian rug, with a profusion of oversize palm and ficus trees in big brass pots adding to its *Arabian Nights Entertainments* theme. The bed was a fantasy come to life, low and the size of a football field, and swathed in filmy lace falling from a ceiling canopy. It sported a velvet comforter patterned in soft blues and greens, with a bank of pillows for a headboard.

Naturally Travis couldn't help but envision Alex there. Alex, her thick braid undone so that her hair was a cloak of gold against the velvet, her bare skin softer, smoother than the fabric, her arms reaching for him....

"Hey, Cross! You there? I mean, it's not like we're discussing anything important here," MacGregor said with ill-concealed sarcasm. "Such as how I'm supposed to explain to the director that instead of busting the bad guys, you robbed them!"

"What the hell was I supposed to do?" Travis demanded. "I'm not even *legal.* As has been recently brought to my attention, I don't even have a current badge. My job was to coordinate—*your* job was to see those guys got picked up. So where were you?"

There was a pregnant pause before Mac said defensively, "Look, I've already told you I'm sorry about that. There was nothing I could do. Both teams were hung up on the bridge. How was I supposed to know the damn thing opens?" He cleared his throat, then said aggressively, "Which still doesn't explain what you thought you were doing."

Travis shifted uncomfortably. "Hey, look—LeClair left before the exchange started to happen. I couldn't see letting the diamonds get away when we don't have a shred of admissible evidence against him. Besides, I've got an idea about how to make this work to our advantage."

"You have a plan?" Mac's tone was openly skeptical.

He had a plan, all right. He was going to get LeClair—one way or another. "Yeah."

Mac sighed. "I guess it won't kill me to listen." Travis could almost see him running an impatient hand through his graying hair. "I guess, if nothing else, there's always the chance LeClair's buyers will get ticked when he fails to deliver and take care of him for us." He gave another gusty sigh. "So where are you, anyway? Give me an address and I'll send a squad car for you so we can discuss your possible strategy."

"I don't think so." Off in the distance, the doorbell rang. Shifting to the left, Travis pushed one booted foot against the swinging door that separated the kitchen from the dining room, opening it a crack. He jockeyed for position until he could see across the dining room, into the living room and beyond to the entry, where Alex had thrown open the door and was ushering a noisy herd of children into the house. The kids immediately began to race around, laughing and talking excitedly and batting at the balloons that were undulating near the ceiling.

"What do you mean, you don't think so?" MacGregor nearly shrieked.

"Hey, Mac, calm down. There are just too many civilians here to risk a pickup," he said, telling himself it was the truth and unwilling to examine too closely any other motives for his sudden reluctance to leave. He was certain it had nothing to do with the lissome blonde collecting coats in the other room.

Serene in the midst of the hubbub, Alex disappeared briefly, then reappeared in answer to another summons by the bell, opening the door to a second wave of boisterous children. She chatted briefly with someone beyond Travis's line of vision, then shut the door. Immediately, she was surrounded by kids, each vying for her attention.

On the other end of the phone, Mac took several audible breaths, before saying distinctly, "Okay, Cross—I'm calm, I'm calm. I'm so calm my blood pressure's in double digits, and you still haven't answered my question. Where... are...you?" He said the last three words very slowly, as if Travis's hearing was impaired—or his intelligence in question.

In the living room, Alex bent over to help one of the latest arrivals, a little boy Travis judged to be five or six, unzip his coat. Her back was to Travis, and the view of her small, rounded derriere sent an unexpected surge of heat shooting through his veins. "I'm in the suburbs celebrating April Fool's Day," he said absently, his eyes riveted on Alex.

What was it about her that got to him so? She wasn't his usual type. She was too classy. Too wholesome. He liked a "hi—goodbye" kind of woman, and Alex had "forever" kind of eyes.

"You're where?" Mac asked, his voice rising once again. "Doing what?" He was back to shrieking.

Travis sighed. "You wouldn't believe me if I told you," he murmured. Louder he said, "Don't sweat it. I just called to tell you I've got the diamonds, I'm in one piece, and I'll meet you as planned at ten o'clock, okay? I'll catch my own ride into town."

"No!" Mac said instantly. "Hold on, Cross! Don't you dare—"

"Gotta go." Ignoring the squawking MacGregor, Travis cradled the receiver of the wall phone.

Alex knew to the minute when Travis hung up the phone. She also knew he'd been watching her. She could feel it like a physical touch. She didn't mind his watching her, exactly; what she did mind, however, was her response to him. Just by looking at her, he made her aware she was a woman—more aware than she'd been in years.

He was just so big and so intense, so...dark. Somewhere along the line, it appeared he had forgotten how to smile. It made her long to ruffle his satiny hair or tickle his ribs or do *something* to lighten the cloak of cynicism that surrounded him. If ever a man needed an attitude adjustment, it was Mr. Travis Cross.

Alex believed life was to be *lived*, a lesson painfully driven home by the sudden, unexpected death of her husband, Stefan. She'd put off their marriage for two years, thinking they'd have forever; she'd learned too late you could only count on today. The experience had left her with a bone-deep conviction that life was to be celebrated, not simply tolerated.

If she had any regrets, it was her childlessness, but it was a minor regret, since all of her friends were more than eager to share their kids with her. She did *not* regret that in the eight years since Stefan's death there had been no man with whom she felt compelled to share her life. She was happy with her life, comfortable with her job, her friends, her home.

But now there was Travis Cross.

It was ridiculous. Outrageous. He was all wrong for her. He had no sense of humor, he swore like a longshoreman and was about as approachable as a porcupine. If all that wasn't bad enough, it appeared he earned his living with the point of a gun, and Alex was a fervent believer in nonviolence.

And yet... and yet, she liked him. He was rude and overbearing, true, but there was just something about him that made every hormone in her body stand up and take notice. Maybe, it was because he was sexy as hell.

Which was a bit of a problem since he appeared to be about as fond of her as he would be of an IRS audit.

A mysterious smile curved her lips. She'd always thrived on challenges, and Travis's apparent dislike would make the next few hours doubly challenging, she decided. Because she was determined to make him lighten up. Of course, that might be cutting off her nose to spite her face. If she found a somber Travis Cross attractive, what would happen when he smiled? Hormone overdose?

"Hey, Auntie Alex." Brandon, her neighbor and best friend Sarah's six-year-old son, tugged on her sweater. "Are we going to play games?"

She looked down fondly at the dark-haired little boy, the youngest of her party goers. "You betcha, kiddo. See those place mats stacked in the corner? Why don't you grab them and bring them to me."

Brandon was off like a shot, beaming with pride as he hurried to do what she asked. Clutching the squares of fabric to his chest he rushed back to her side. "Great," she told him. Of all her various courtesy nieces and nephews, Brandon was her favorite. Clapping her hands, she drew the attention of the other children. "Okay, everybody, move back and clear a space. It's time to play musical chairs or, in this case, musical squares. Brandon, you lay the place mats out in a big circle. Everybody get on a square, although I'm sure you guys already know we're one square short, which is how the game is played. I'll handle the music and—" she paused, shooting Travis a look that was an obvious dare "—Mr. Cross will be the judge."

Travis couldn't have looked more horrified if she'd suggested the two of them play strip poker in front of the kids. Still straddling the doorway, he didn't move an inch, just stared at her as if she'd lost her mind. He cleared his throat. "I'm afraid I don't—"

"This is easy," Alex assured him, her eyes dancing with mischief. "There are fourteen kids and thirteen place mats. When the music stops, the person who's not on a square is out. We take away one square and we do it again. Your job is to settle any disputes if two players both claim they were the first on the square. I know you can handle it."

He still didn't move. "Why can't you do it?" he asked, his reluctance obvious.

"Because," Alex said reasonably, "the stereo's in the corner where I can't see clearly."

"Well, why don't I take care of the stereo and you be the judge?" he asked, then immediately answered his own question. "Oh, I know. It's like your car. Nobody drives your car, nobody touches your stereo?"

Alex hadn't thought of that. "Right." It was a better reason than anything she could have come up with.

For a minute, Travis looked as if he was going to say something more. Then, remembering the children, he thought better of it, and with a nonchalant shrug, moved into the room, taking his place just outside the ring of waiting kids. He turned and looked at Alex. "Go for it," he said tersely. Suppressing a smile, Alex did.

The first few rounds went smoothly, with only minor altercations about who was in and who was out. By the time they got to the final round, the contest was between Brandon and a slightly older but considerably bigger boy named Sean.

The two boys took up their positions, the rest of the kids waiting expectantly. Alex turned the music on. Travis watched. Round and round the lone place mat in the middle of the floor the two boys marched. The music stopped. Brandon jumped. Sean jumped, too, but because he was taller, he had a distinct advantage. Planting both feet on the square while the smaller boy was still in midair, he immediately began to chant, "I won! I won! I won!"

Brandon knocked into him, yelling, "Did not! Did not! He cheated, Mr. Cross!" The two tussled for a minute, then turned to Travis, both claiming victory and demanding he settle the dispute.

Travis looked over the heads of the children at Alex, his expression clearly conveying his displeasure at the situation he suddenly found himself in. She gave him a commiserating smile, but stayed where she was, refusing to come to his aid.

The decision rested in his hands. Travis stifled a curse. The problem was that Sean was a bully. Twelve rounds of play had made that clear, and Travis hated bullies. He *wanted* to declare Brandon the winner. He had a soft spot for underdogs, and the scrappy little boy was definitely that. But unfortunately, Sean had won *this* round fair and square. Shooting a last quelling glance at Alex, Travis directed his gaze at the two youngsters and shrugged. "I'm sorry, buddy," he said to Brandon. "Sean won."

Sean beamed and once more began to chant, "I won!" Brandon's shoulders sagged. Travis longed for a drink and wondered where Alex kept the spare key for the Ferrari. He'd already searched the kitchen. The den, maybe?

Before he had time for further speculation, Alex had given Sean his prize, picked up the place mats and had all the children embroiled in a quick game of beanbag toss, which Sean managed to win, too. Telling himself he was being ridiculous, Travis still couldn't suppress a sense of disgust at the overbearing child's victory. At least the kid didn't win the third game. Travis experienced a perverse twinge of pleasure when Sean pinned the tail between the donkey's eyeballs instead of the other end.

"Last game," Alex declared, picking up a tangle of intertwined nylon rope. On one end, the ropes were tied to one of the legs of the dining-room table. She passed out the other rope ends to each of the children. When there were two ends left in her hand, she handed one to Travis.

Looking her in the eye, he said, "I don't play games." He handed it back.

Alex refused to take it. She raised one brow. "Never?"

His expression didn't change. "Never."

"Well," she said cheerfully, "you do now. One of the kids is sick and it will ruin the game if all the ropes aren't used. Please?"

Travis had never understood how Helen of Troy could have sent men to their deaths with just a word. Now he did. "Fine," he said with a long-suffering sigh. "Give me the rope." As he took it from her outstretched hand, he knew he was probably making a grave mistake.

He was right. The game consisted of untangling the ropes without letting your end loose, which meant everyone was immediately jumbled together, twisting and turning, crawling over and under each other, each vying to be the first to get their line untangled and reach the dining-room table.

The minute Alex said "go," Travis was in trouble. One minute he was standing upright. The next, a rope snaked around his ankles and someone pulled and suddenly he was flat on his back on the carpet with an army of small bodies scrambling over him. Sharp little elbows and knees jabbed him in the stomach. Size-two shoes scaled his chest. Childish shrieks rang in his ears.

Afraid he might inadvertently hurt someone, he controlled the urge to throw off his mini-attackers, concentrating instead on giving a helpful boost to anyone who got too close to the more vulnerable parts of his anatomy. Carefully dislodging a small hand clutching his nose, he decided he was doing pretty well until someone fell flat on top of him and his face was blanketed in a cloud of fragrant golden hair.

It didn't take Albert Einstein to figure out this was not a child. Brushing away the clinging strands of silky hair clinging to his eyelashes, he stared up into Alex's big brown eyes, which were about five inches from his own. The two of them stared at each other. He could feel every soft curve pressed against him like a brand. He could also see from the way her eyes darkened as they gazed at each other that she was aware of him, too. The minutes spun out. To his chagrin, Travis could feel his body hardening in the kind of involuntary response he hadn't had in years. But this was worse, because now he was a man. Which was becoming more and more obvious with every second that passed.

Alex noticed it, too. Her lips parted on a rush of breath, a surprised look appearing on her face as she gazed down at him. "Oh, my."

To his utter mortification, Travis felt a tide of red creep up his neck. What the hell was wrong with him? He was behaving with all the polish of a horny teenager at his first make-out party! "I—uh—"

"Wow, Auntie Alex! This is really rad," Brandon said, his small face appearing over Alex's shoulder. "Isn't it totally tubular, Mr. Cross?"

Tubular was *one* way of putting it, Travis decided. Before he could formulate an answer, Brandon was gone. He looked at Alex.

She looked back. A sweet smile curved her lips. "Having fun, Mr. Cross?"

"Fun is not precisely how I'd describe it, Ms. Wright," Travis gritted out. *Sexual torture was more like it.* He willed his body to behave itself.

Her expression suspiciously innocent, Alex gave the slightest of shrugs. "Feels good to me," she whispered for him alone, then her tone changed to a lighthearted, "Well, gotta go." She immediately rolled away.

Travis knew he had to have heard her wrong. She couldn't have said what he thought she'd said. Could she? Before he had time to give it further thought, a little boy wearing what had to be size-ten tennis shoes mistook Travis's stomach for a launching pad. With a yelp of pain, Travis clutched his middle and bolted upright, towing several little bodies attached to ropes with him. He stumbled backward, bumping into the dining-room table. "Okay," he roared. "That's it."

Brandon immediately started jumping up and down. "You won, Mr. Cross, you won!"

With a sense of shock, Travis looked at the rope in his hand, glanced around and realized the child was right. Somehow, while he was just lying there, everyone else had done the work of freeing him. With the force of a laser beam, his brilliant blue eyes locked on Alex. For once, the elegant Ms. Wright didn't look quite so elegant. Her hair tumbled in gleaming strands to her waist, her cheeks were flushed, her eyes glowing, and her lips were parted in an unconscious invitation as she strove to catch her breath. She looked, Travis thought instantly, like a woman who'd just spent a satisfying session in bed.

Just the idea nearly destroyed him, but he refused to let it defeat him. He'd show Alex she wasn't the only one who could be calm and cool and composed. As far as that went, it was about her turn to blush. "So, Ms. Wright," he said in a husky voice ripe with suggestion, "what do I get for winning?"

Alex would have needed one foot in the grave to mistake his meaning. It had the opposite effect on her from what Travis intended, however. She didn't feel the least bit embarrassed or intimidated, which was obviously his intention. Far from it. Although he didn't know it, she had achieved her goal. The man was *playing* with her, even if he hadn't realized it yet. The problem was, if a somber Travis Cross was attractive, this slightly rakish version with the knowing gleam in his deep blue eyes was positively dangerous, just as she'd feared. Deciding it was definitely time to take control of the conversation, she answered his question. "You get something for winning that will make your taste buds water and your lips pucker up for more." She gave him what she hoped was a sultry look.

"Oh, yeah?" The gleam in his eyes intensified.

Reaching behind her for the bag that held the prizes, she picked it up and delved inside. "Yeah." Approaching him, she extended her hand.

He looked down. "What's that?" His brow slightly creased, he stared in mild puzzlement at the bright circle of multicolored candy on a stick.

Alex stared up into his eyes, her own twinkling. "Why, Mr. Cross, don't you recognize it? It's your prize. An all-day sucker."

For an instant, she thought she might have gone too far. If looks could kill, the one Travis turned on her should have made her fall to the floor. "You know, lady," he said in a voice only she could hear, "I owe you one."

Alex didn't miss a beat. "Well, as long as I'm on your list, anyway, you might as well owe me two. You can come and help me get the food together for these Munchkins." Before he could demur, she turned and addressed the children. "What do you say, kids? Are you ready for cake and ice cream?" The chorus of cheers left no doubt as to the next step in the party's progress.

Travis had to admit she was as smooth an operator as anyone he'd ever encountered. Without knowing quite how she managed it, he soon found himself up to his elbows dishing out chocolate-ripple ice cream while Alex cut and served the cake, which, he belatedly realized, had been the large rectangle he'd earlier seen her remove from the car.

Everyone was soon served and busily eating away. Alex gave a sigh of contentment and turned to him, her manner relaxed and friendly. "Thanks for the help. How about a beer? You've earned it."

"I've earned more than that." The minute the words were out of his mouth, Travis wished he could recall them. He thought he'd been all through this, but apparently his libido was on a different wavelength than his brain. "Just forget I said that. And, yes, I'd like a beer."

In a completely natural gesture, Alex leaned close and gave him a quick hug. "Don't worry about it."

Damn her for that hug. How was he supposed to convince his suddenly hyperactive sex drive to behave itself if she wouldn't keep her hands to herself? Wordlessly, he accepted the beer she handed him. He took a long pull of the cold, soothing beverage, hoping it would help to calm his rebellious body. In an attempt to help the process along, he looked for a diversion.

He found it when he looked around the table and realized they were shy one small party goer. Brandon. Scanning the room, Travis was just in time to see a small body attached to a mop of dark hair whip out the front door. Without a word to Alex, who was busy getting Sean seconds of cake, he followed.

A quick glance at the well-illuminated front porch told Travis the child wasn't there, but a faint squeaking from around the far left corner hinted at his location. Travis crossed to the side porch, which was cloaked in shadows.

After squeezing his eyes shut for a minute to help them adjust to the change in light, he took a look around. To his left was a porch swing, hung from the ceiling by heavy chains. As he watched, it swayed. Moving soundlessly, no slight feat in cowboy boots, he approached.

Brandon was huddled in one corner of the swing, head resting against the back, short legs swaying two feet above the ground. "Hey, buddy," Travis said softly, not wanting to startle the child. "Mind if I join you?"

Brandon gave a halfhearted shrug. "Sure."

Travis sat, leaned his head back in imitation of the child and stretched out his long legs, setting the swing in motion.

"Someday I'm gonna be big enough to do that. Auntie Alex said."

"I imagine she's right." Travis took a swallow of beer, then observed casually, "This was a good idea. It was getting too noisy in there."

"Yeah, and that rotten Sean stole the rose off my cake. I hate him. He thinks he can do any old thing he wants because he's bigger than me."

Travis thought about that. "Well, kid, there's a lot of that in the world. You just have to learn to roll with the punches and bide your time, because eventually the good guys do get their chance. Sometimes it just takes a little longer."

"I s'pose." He cocked his head, looking at Travis with heightened interest. "Y'know, that's what Milton Monster always tells Jason Who's Becoming, too."

"Milton Monster?" Travis inquired.

"Yep. He's in my favoritest book, *The Great Beyond.* See, he's this really rad monster who helps this boy named Jason learn about growing up and how not to make a lot of dumb mistakes. Jason's an orphan who lives in this neat world called The Beyond, and they have all these cool adventures while Jason tries to find where he belongs."

"Umm," Travis said neutrally. "Sounds interesting. Does it have good pictures?"

"The coolest," Brandon said decisively. "Auntie Alex says—" his face screwed up as he struggled to remember "—that it's the best kind of book 'cuz it's a thinking book. That means," he explained earnestly, "that there's a fun story but also a mural, too."

One corner of Travis's mouth curved in the dark before he corrected gently, "I think you mean moral, buddy."

"That's what I said. Anyway, Auntie Alex got it for me, which is pretty cool for a girl."

"Oh." *He should have known.* "I guess you think Alex is pretty smart, don't you?"

"Yep. When I get bigger, I'm gonna marry her. That is...unless...Are you gonna marry her, Mr. Cross?"

Travis choked on his beer. It was a moment before he could speak. "Uh, no. Marrying Alex isn't exactly what I had in mind. And Brandon? Call me Travis, okay?"

"Okay. But you're Auntie Alex's boyfriend, aren't you, Travis? She's never had one, not since her husband died."

Travis digested this. Alex had been married? He didn't know why it surprised him. She was a beautiful woman, with no glaring personality faults—except the way she drove. When he thought about it, he decided what was strange was that she *didn't* have some guy hanging around. Feeling rather foolish pumping a kid, he nonetheless found himself asking, "Did Alex's husband die recently?"

"Naw," Brandon said breezily. "It was a long time ago, before I was born. I heard my mom tell my dad that's why it's such a shame that all the guys Auntie Alex meets at her job are so wimpy. My mom says she needs a *real* man, not those stuffy college teachers."

"You don't say." What she *needed* was a keeper; someone to keep her from debating with armed men, someone to keep her from inviting potentially dangerous strangers into her home. Someone to keep her off the roads...

Brandon continued. "Yep. And when me and my dad went to the confession stand for a hot dog at the ball game, I heard him tell his friend Wally that any guy smart enough to marry Auntie Alex would get an angel in his life with a bobfire in his bed. What's a bobfire, Travis? Is that what happens on Sunday morning when my parents lock their bedroom door and won't let me or my sister in?"

Travis briefly debated trying to explain the difference between confession and concession and finally decided that in the interest of time, ignoring the boy's creative vocabulary would be his wisest course of action. Likewise, he had no intention of discussing Alex's potential flammability with a six-year-old, much less what went on in Brandon's parent's bedroom on Sunday mornings—or any morning, for that matter.

He searched for something to say. Anything to say. And then inspiration struck. "Why don't you ask Alex, buddy? After all, she knows everything."

The boy sighed. "Naw. She won't tell me, either. She said I had to wait until pubatory."

Pubatory? Travis took another swig of beer and racked his brain. "Uh, Brandon, I think that's puberty."

"Naw, it's not. What it is, is dumb. Nobody'll tell me anything. How am I supposed to learn if nobody'll tell me anything?" He sighed deeply, rubbing a hand wearily across his eyes.

"I don't know," Travis admitted. He didn't know what else to say. The kid had a point, but it was hardly Travis's place to enlighten him. Dr. Ruth he was not. Deciding in this instance discretion was the better part of valor, he concentrated on rocking the swing in a constant, soothing rhythm. After a little while, he felt a warm weight against his side. Looking down with surprise, he found Brandon cuddled against him. "Hey, buddy," he said softly.

"I don't feel so good," the little boy confided. "I have a pain under my hair."

Travis couldn't help the smile that tugged at his lips. "Then we'll just sit here real quiet," he said. "That's what I do when my hair hurts."

"Okay."

In complete understanding, the two of them closed their eyes and let the night close around them.

It wasn't until Sarah arrived that Alex realized Brandon was missing. Although Travis's departure had been impossible to overlook, Brandon was known to curl up in a corner on occasion, and in the midst of all the kids' roughhousing after the cake and ice cream, she hadn't realized the child was gone, too. Assuring Sarah she'd find her son, she checked both upstairs and down, telling herself not to panic, that Travis Cross wasn't some kind of diabolical fiend who would hurt an innocent child.

When she didn't find Brandon or Travis inside, she tried the porch, heading toward the swing on the side porch, which was one of the child's favorite spots. Hurrying along, she rounded the corner only to bump into a wicker table that was not in its usual place.

"Shh." Travis's voice came out of the darkness.

Thank God. Brandon, it appeared, wasn't the only one who liked the swing. Pushing the table back where it belonged, she whispered, "Travis? Have you seen a little boy with dark hair?"

"You mean Brandon? He's right here. He's asleep. I don't know very much about kids, but he feels awfully hot to me."

By this time Alex's eyes had adjusted to the dim light. With the moonlight spilling onto the porch, the small outline of Brandon snuggled up to the broader shadow that was Travis was quite clear. Stepping closer with the lithe grace Travis found so attractive, she knelt at his feet and carefully placed her hand on the little boy's forehead. "You're right," she said, touched by his concern. Mentally she apologized to him for her earlier moment of doubt. "He does feel warm. I hope he's not coming down with a cold." Tenderly she stroked the child's flushed cheek before rocking back on her heels. "Everyone else has gone. His mother's here, but it seems a shame to wake him. They only live next door. Would you mind carrying him home?"

"No," Travis said quickly. "Not at all." In fact, he welcomed the activity. The prospect of carrying a fifty-pound kid a few hundred feet was a lot less disturbing than having Alex kneeling at his feet.

"I'll just go get Sarah," she said, rising.

He breathed a sigh of relief at her departure and came to his feet, the child cradled easily in his arms. This was getting way out of hand. First Alex had gotten under his skin, then the kid.

He had a job to do—a score to settle with LeClair. It was ridiculous to be standing here in the damn moonlight feeling the way he did, wondering what it would be like if he and Alex and the child were a real family. That sort of stuff was fairy-tale fluff, and he'd quit believing in happily-ever-after a long time ago.

When Alex reappeared with a short dark-haired woman who he assumed was Brandon's mom, he gave the two women a curt nod, then wordlessly followed them down the steps. In no time at all, Brandon was tucked into his own bed and Travis and Alex were back at her house.

For the first time in years, Alex felt uncertain how to proceed. The sight of Brandon clasped in the arms of big, tough Travis Cross had affected her strangely. For some reason, there was an ache in the region of her heart, a vague sense of longing unfamiliar to her. Still, she felt uncomfortable saying nothing, so she settled for "Thanks," giving a gentle squeeze to Travis's muscular arm.

To her surprise, he jerked away as if he'd been burned. "Don't worry about it," he said abruptly. "I was just doing what I had to do so I could get the hell out of here. Do you suppose we could go? I mean, you did promise when the party was over we'd go."

Alex refused to take offense. Instinct told her it was what he expected, and she rarely did the expected. Studying him, she took in his aggressive stance, his legs spread wide, his arms crossed against his broad chest, and she suddenly had a pretty good idea of what was eating him. She didn't imagine it was good for his big, bad spy-guy image to be caught cuddling on a porch swing with a little kid. She was smart enough not to share the observation, however. Instead, all she said was, "You're right, I did. Let me get my purse." Retrieving it from the other room, she returned to

he kitchen, waltzed past where he stood and headed out the
door.

He followed her out, pausing on the steps. "Aren't you
forgetting something?" he asked caustically.

"Ah," she smiled. "You must mean the keys. Nope.
Observe." Raising her fingers to her mouth, she gave a
short, ear-splitting whistle, which was answered immediately by a high-pitched beeping noise from the bushes. Following the sound, Alex crossed the yard, waded into the
underbrush and stooped to retrieve her keys. Turning, she
grinned at Travis. "If I have a fault, it's that I'm always
losing my keys, so my brother got me this last Christmas.
An unloseable key ring. All the locksmiths in town went into
mourning." She moved to the car, unlocked the passenger
door, then went around to the driver's side and did the
same. "Coming?"

Travis shook his head as he walked toward the car. "If I
was keeping score, lady, the keys would be number three."

Alex looked at him brightly. "Is there a magic number?
What happens if I hit it?"

He shook his head some more. "Trust me, you don't want
to know." He pulled open the car door. "I never thought I'd
hear myself actually saying this, but would you just get in
the car and drive? Please?"

Alex snapped him a mock-solemn salute. "At your com-
mand," she said, sliding into the car. The engine turned over
at a touch of the key.

Travis got in, wisely fastening his seat belt *before* he
closed the door. The instant the door clicked shut, he was
thrown forward against the harness as she put the car into
reverse and roared backward out of the drive. "Do you
think this time you could keep it under eighty?" he yelled
over the scream of the engine, cringing as they barely missed

the corner post of the carport. His stomach lodged in his throat.

Alex hit the brakes, shifted in a blur of motion into first, pushed the accelerator to the floor and ran through the gears. In seconds they were hurtling down the dark country road, the speedometer hovering at seventy-five. Travis was vastly relieved when they made the freeway, telling himself there was less chance of meeting his maker with three lanes of pavement for Alex to maneuver in. Boeing, he decided as he watched the scenery fly by, should put her under contract. The big, Seattle-based airplane manufacturer could use her to measure the nerves of their test pilots. Of course, if they did, they probably wouldn't have anybody left to fly...

It was the longest, quickest ride of his life. In record time, they rumbled to a stop in front of the address he'd given for his hotel, Alex eyeing the six-story building dubiously. Forty years ago the structure might have been elegant, but time had not been kind. Dwarfed by a pair of skyscrapers on either side, the small, squat brick building bordered on seedy.

Government work must not pay very well, Alex decided with a pang. For some reason, the thought of leaving Travis here was disturbing. "You know," she said carefully, not wanting to offend his pride, "my house is awfully big for one person. You'd be more than welcome if you'd like to stay there."

Travis looked at her in surprise, then had to stifle a laugh at the irony when he identified her dismay as she sat peering out at the old hotel. My God. The woman's driving was enough to scare even Stephen King, and she was worried about him staying in a shabby hotel? Bemused, he shook his head slightly at the vagaries of her personality. "Thanks," he said, "but I'm expected here." He unlatched his seat belt.

"Oh." Tearing her gaze from the run-down hotel, Alex turned to face him. Their eyes met across the shadowy interior of the Ferrari. "Well." Releasing the steering wheel, she offered him her right hand. "I guess this is goodbye, then. It's been . . . interesting."

Travis took her hand. It felt smooth and fragile, the skin incredibly soft against his own callused palm, and holding it set off an avalanche of desire in his gut. He stared at her, looking at her dark brown eyes, her complexion as flawless as whipped cream, her smooth, pink lips. "Well, hell," he said under his breath. A moment later, he gave in to temptation and tugged her close, claiming her mouth with his.

Alex gasped at the unexpected contact, passion exploding in her veins as her lips and Travis's meshed like a pair of interlocking puzzle pieces. His mouth was warm and firm, the hands now holding both of hers pressed to his chest were hard and hot, and kissing him was the most exciting thing she'd ever done. She swayed, leaning closer, lost in the moment, lost in Travis Cross.

He tasted exotic, a combination of ice cream, danger and beer. She could feel his heart thundering beneath her fingertips, feel the heat rolling off him like a furnace as her palms pressed against the soft cotton T-shirt stretched over his taut chest. Pulling free of his grip, she ran her hands up his neck to the back of his head and clasped him tighter, ignoring the steering wheel pressing into her side and the stick shift jabbing her thigh as she tried to scoot closer. She felt as if she was going up in flames, and although she suspected she was going to be mortified later at her feverish behavior, right now it didn't matter. Nothing mattered except getting closer to the source of such pleasure.

And then, to her dismay, it was over, their incendiary kiss ending as precipitously as it had begun when Travis abruptly pulled away. She bit back a protest, her eyes fluttering open to lock on Travis's blue ones, which appeared black and opaque in the dim light. She could read nothing there. "Travis?" she whispered, taking a shuddering breath.

He wrenched open the door, a desperate man bent on escape. "Thanks for the ride, Alex. I hate to run, but I've got to go."

She couldn't let him leave like this. "Wait!" With a restraining hand to his arm, she momentarily stopped his determined retreat. Digging frantically around in the Ferrari's center console, she came up with a rectangle of heavily embossed paper and struggled for composure. "Here," she said, handing him one of her cards. She gave him a pale imitation of her usual serene smile. "If you're ever in town and need to make a quick getaway, don't be afraid to call."

"Yeah, sure," Travis said, pocketing the card as he scrambled out of the low-slung car. Slamming the door, he started to walk away, then stopped and turned back, stooping to scowl at her through the tinted glass, waiting while she pressed a button and the window slid down. "Hey," he said, squatting down to eye level. "Don't drive so damn fast, okay?" Then he swiveled on his heel and was gone.

"Right," Alex murmured softly to the empty street. An abandoned section of newsprint fluttered in the gutter, caught by a puff of breeze. "You take care, too, Mr. Secret Agent Cross."

Three

"Sarah's late again," Connie Slater observed, lounging back in one of Alex's ultracomfortable kitchen chairs.

"What an earth-shattering observation," DeeDee Kelly said from the other side of the table. The fiftyish blonde fluffed her youthful platinum ponytail and sighed dramatically. "But then, you're the only woman I know, Constance, who still thinks that the missionary style refers to a fashion statement."

Despite herself, Alex smiled, knowing there was no real malice behind DeeDee's caustic words. She'd been playing bridge with both women for the past two years and had long since figured out that their bickering was simply a quirk of their friendship.

Pouring white wine into a quartet of glasses, she paused for a minute to look fondly around her kitchen. It felt good to be back. She'd arrived home only the night before last, having taken some personal time to visit her brother and his family in Denver after the Arizona language conference she'd attended. As always, her visit with Rick and Sally had been great, and she'd had a wonderful time with her nieces. But still, there was no place like home.

The back door swung open and Sarah Nelson, Brandon's mother and their fourth for bridge, came hurrying in. "Finally! I thought I'd never get here." She bumped the door shut with a shapely hip and set a sinfully rich-looking chocolate cake on the counter next to a platter of veggies and low-cal dip.

"What happened to you?" Alex asked, taking in her best friend and former college roommate's harried state. She took Sarah's jacket and handed her a glass of wine.

"Don't ask! It's been h-e-double-toothpicks at my house for the past two weeks. Never, *ever* have two kids with the chicken pox at the same time. Believe me, it's the pits." Sarah sank gratefully into the chair next to DeeDee's and took an appreciative sip from her glass. "Umm... fantastic."

"Chicken pox?" Alex handed the other two women their wine, then took her own glass and sat down. Connie began to shuffle. "You mean Brandon and Lizabeth have been sick?"

Sarah gave Alex a knowing grin. "Relax, Auntie Alex. They're fine. I'm the one who may never be the same. I've read the adventures of Milton Monster to the kids so many times I could scream. I wish the author would hurry up with a sequel—I could use a change." Despite the words, Sarah looked remarkably cheerful. "We were pretty lucky, actually. Lizabeth's rash was mild, and although Brandon still itches like crazy, except for the first few days he really hasn't felt too bad. He goes back to school tomorrow. The only really awful part was that he broke out the day after your party, so I had to contact all the kids' parents. They were all pretty understanding, though. It seems chicken pox is going around.''

Alex gave Sarah a teasing smile. "I guess I picked the right time to be gone.''

Sarah stuck out her tongue. "Yep, truly great timing, Alex. There were several times I would have killed for your help. You know how Brandon adores you. Brad swears the three most overworked words in Brandon's vocabulary are 'Auntie Alex says.'''

DeeDee, who didn't have a maternal bone in her well-preserved body, said pointedly, "I hope that's the end of the Mary Poppins Report, because I want to hear all about Alex's conference." Her eyes drilled into Alex. "So? Did you meet any men? Have any wild encounters you want to share?" She wiggled her darkened brows suggestively.

"Hussy," Connie said primly, dealing out the cards with furious efficiency.

Alex exchanged an amused glance with Sarah as all four women began arranging their cards. "Sorry, Dee. I still haven't met Prince Charming."

Sarah's eyes sparkled mischievously. "Really? What about that hunk who carried Brandon home the night of your party? I've been dying to hear where he came from ever since he rose up off your porch looking like a cross between Mel Gibson and a young Sean Connery."

Like a bloodhound catching a scent, DeeDee's head snapped up. "I knew it! Alex, you sly puss, you've been holding out on us," she accused. Curiosity glowed in her eyes like a neon sign. "So who is he? Is he really gorgeous?"

Even though she'd just spent two weeks trying to forget the torrid way she'd behaved in his arms, a picture of Travis Cross formed instantly in Alex's mind. She envisioned his rich, dark hair, his brilliant blue eyes, his thick, inky lashes shadowing strong cheeks. And when she recalled how he'd looked just before they parted, the passion of their kiss still stamped on his lips, she couldn't stop the way her pulse sped up.

"So?" DeeDee persisted. "Is he gorgeous or not? Come on, Alex, give!"

"I can answer that," Sarah said smugly. "You know how much I love Brad, but if I *was* going to fall off the straight and narrow, this guy would be well worth a tumble."

"Sarah!" Alex hissed.

Sarah raised her hands, affecting a look of injured innocence belied by the laughter twinkling in her eyes. "Hey, married is not synonymous with dead, Alex, and the guy was a real heartbreaker. On a scale of one to ten," she added with a wicked smile, "I'd give him a twelve."

"Alex?" DeeDee prompted.

Alex gave a long-suffering sigh. "Oh, all right." She tossed Sarah a narrow look, then said defiantly, "A nine. I imagine if he ever smiled, he'd be a ten. Satisfied?"

"My Eldon's a ten," Connie offered proudly.

"We're not talking shoe size here, Con," DeeDee said scathingly. "Now, be quiet, I'm not done with Alex. Did you meet him at the university? Is he a teacher? Maybe an expert in . . . sex ed?"

Alex groaned. "No, he's not a teacher." She could see there was no way out of this. Better just to get it over with. "We met at the mall. He had car trouble and needed a lift, so I offered to take him into Seattle after the party. That's it," Alex added firmly. "Are we going to play bridge?"

"Give it up, Al," Sarah advised. "Brandon says your Travis was asking questions about the other men you date, that he even mentioned marriage. Now, that doesn't sound like somebody whose only concern was a ride."

Alex had more than a sneaking suspicion Brandon had the conversation turned around. She couldn't visualize taciturn Travis Cross confiding in a kindergartner. More likely, Brandon had done the talking and Travis had learned more than he'd bargained for.

"All I did was give the man a ride to his hotel," Alex repeated. Despite her offhand manner, a pang of longing shot through her as she continued to think about Travis. Appalled, she dismissed it as ridiculous. After all, she'd only spent a few hours with the man and it was unlikely she'd ever see him again. And even if she did, the way he earned his living disqualified him as anyone with whom she'd willingly get involved. It would be emotional suicide to fall in love with a man whose job was so dangerous. She'd already lost someone she loved to violence; she wasn't going through that again.

"You know, Alex," Sarah said gently, "it's past time you started looking around. I mean, there have been plenty of guys who've been interested. You need to get interested back. You can't live alone forever."

"Sarah's right," DeeDee said. "Face it, sweetie, if we filmed your love life it wouldn't even rate PG. Bambi had more fun than you do, and half the time people were shooting at him."

"Thank you, Siskel and Ebert," Alex said dryly. "Look, maybe you're right, but Travis Cross isn't for me. Besides, chances are I'll never see him again." She assured herself that didn't bother her, dismissing the slight ache around her heart that suggested otherwise as heartburn from the wine, and sent DeeDee and Sarah a glance that warned the discussion was over. "Let's play cards. I'll open with two clubs."

"Well, break out the Midol," DeeDee said under her breath, but at least she focused on her cards. She frowned. "I'll pass."

Sarah's eyes met Alex's. "Two hearts," she said meaningfully.

"Three spades," Connie said next, before unexpectedly reaching over to give Alex a commiserating pat on the shoulder. "It's too bad the hunk dumped you, dear, but it's like I always say. If at first you don't succeed, try, try, try again."

Alex had a sudden urge to toss her cards in the air.

High above the Rockies, the commercial jet dipped and lunged, buffeted by strong, swirling winds. Travis shifted in his seat, trying futilely to find a comfortable position for his six-foot-two frame in a space designed for Pygmies. The only saving grace about the late-night flight from JFK to Seattle was that it had been underbooked, so at least he had three seats all to himself. Which was good, because a nagging headache had been plaguing him for hours and he was definitely not in the mood for company.

Belatedly remembering the aspirin he'd purchased in the concourse before boarding, he reached into his jacket pocket and pulled out the bottle. His eyes narrowed as he saw the business card struck to its side. Peeling the white rectangle away from the plastic container, he smoothed out a crease before turning it over to read the name.

Alexis Wright. He'd forgotten she'd given him her card. He ran a finger over the embossed printing. Alex, with the golden braid and the satin lips and a smile some men would happily die for.

He snapped the cap off the aspirin bottle and palmed three tablets, tossing them down with the last of his scotch.

Reclining the seat back, he bunched the undersize airline pillow beneath his head.

Alex. Funny that he should be reminded of her now, when he was on his way back to Seattle. As much as it galled him to admit it, she'd nearly done him in with that single, searing kiss they'd shared. For the first time since his teenage years, a mere kiss had kicked his libido into overdrive and managed to keep it there for days. There'd even been several nights when his dreams had been on the hot side of feverish.

An image formed in his mind of a curvy little derriere, of breasts as round and soft as peaches, of incredibly long, elegant legs, of whisper-soft hair gilded like sunshine.

His finger traced over the phone number on the card.

For all she drove like a maniac, Alex *was* damn sexy. Maybe, since he was going to be in town for a while anyway, he should consider giving her a call....

He stuffed the card back into his jeans pocket as if it had burned him. What the hell was he thinking? He had a job to do, a mission to accomplish, and here he was mooning over some dame. There was no way around it; the woman was trouble—hell, just thinking about her made him crazy!

He crossed his arms over his chest and closed his eyes, resolutely vowing not to give her another thought. He was so damned tired, anyway, and this was as good an excuse as any to force himself to clear his mind and try to get some rest. Settling back, he gave in to the urge to yawn....

He must have dozed. One moment he could feel the motion of the plane around him, and the next, he was dreaming, transported back in time to a littered New Jersey alleyway behind a handful of upscale stores.

With a swiftly escalating sense of panic, he knew both that he'd actually been in this place in the past—and that he'd had this dream before; the setting was as familiar to him as his own face. LeClair's—the red brick store was the gangster cum jeweler's, and there, at the far end of the alley...

His feet dragged leadenly as he walked reluctantly toward the large metal dumpster. Beads of sweat popped out on his clammy skin, dampening his hair, saturating his shirt. Horror stabbed like knives through his gut.

He knew he had to look inside the container; something—or was it someone?—was lost and it was his job to find him, but a shrill voice in his head warned him away.

He ignored it, grasping the rusty lid; the metal was ice cold between his fingers and the hinges shrieked a protest as he slowly, slowly lifted.

With an iron will, he forced himself not to look away, not to blink, not to flinch, as he stared at the sprawled body of his best friend and fellow agent Joel Gibson lying dead in a bed of garbage. And as he fought to contain the scream of anguish building in his chest, Joel's corpse opened its eyes to stare accusingly at him. "Your fault, Travis," he said. "It's your fault I'm dead."

The horrible words sent shards of pain splintering through his aching head.

He stumbled back and turned to run, but pain exploded in his right thigh, and he knew, even before the sound of the gunshot reached his ears, that he'd been hit.

In the next moment, the dreamscape altered drastically, the pain in his thigh magically disappearing, the alley closing in around him to become a narrow, shabby elevator. He looked wildly around, trying to get his bearings, desperate to escape, sensing a new danger but not recognizing it yet.

The elevator shuddered to a stop. The doors creaked open. The hair on the back of his neck tingled as he stepped cautiously into the hall. It was dark, so dark; only a single weak bulb burned in the cheap overhead fixture. It was familiar...so familiar, but where the hell was he?

And then he knew. He was at the shabby hotel in Seattle where Alexis Wright had left him. He was going to meet Mac and explain his plan, but something had gone wrong.

From down the hallway came the muted swish of a door opening. A foreshadowing of danger iced down his spine. Adrenaline poured through his veins. A heartbeat later, the two men from the shopping center burst into the corridor and raced toward him, guns blazing. Bullets smashed into the crumbling walls, sending chunks of plaster flying. The acrid bite of cordite permeated the air.

Oh, God! He didn't want to die! He hurled himself to the ground, his hand flashing to the semiautomatic tucked in the waistband of his pants even as he rolled for cover. His heart thundered in his chest. He took aim and fired—

"Sir?"

Travis jerked awake to find the stewardess standing over him, her pretty face wreathed in a polite smile.

"I'm sorry to wake you, but we'll be landing soon. The captain has called for all seats to be returned to the upright position."

Travis stared at her blankly, willing his heart to stop racing, trying to ignore the nausea churning through his gut. His head was pounding, his mouth tasted as if he'd sucked on an ashtray, and every bone in his body ached. In short, he felt like hell.

He realized the stewardess was waiting, staring at him with an expression of concern. From somewhere he dredged up a smile. "It's okay," he said, leaning forward to allow the seat up as she'd requested.

"Are you feeling all right?" she asked solicitously.

Travis felt the perspiration bead at his nape and trickle between his shoulder blades. He wondered how he could be sweating when the temperature inside the plane had to be below zero, but still he answered, "I'm fine."

She glanced at him uncertainly. "Well, if you're sure..."

"Very." Their eyes met, his closed blue gaze as eloquent as any words in expressing his wish that she move on. The woman flushed slightly, then hurried away down the aisle.

Travis turned and stared blindly out the window. God, what was going on? What was wrong with him? He hadn't dreamed about finding Joel for months. And as for the other—why should he dream about the attempt on his life the night Alex had dropped him off *now?* After all, things had worked out fine. With his unerring instinct for trouble, Mac had arrived on the scene with the police just seconds after the shooting had started, and LeClair's lackeys had promptly been arrested. Hell, the purported reason for Travis's return to Seattle was to testify at their trial.

Clamping down on his rampaging emotions, he took deep even breaths, bringing his skyrocketing pulse rate under control, forcing himself to think, needing to be certain that the nightmares were simply what they seemed and not his subconscious warning him of something he'd overlooked when devising his plan to get the mastermind responsible for Joel's murder.

But try as he might, he couldn't see anyplace he'd slipped up. As he'd explained to Mac, the attempt on his life was actually a twofold break. It showed the extent of LeClair's determination to get the diamonds back, while revealing that somebody within the Department was passing the man information—how else would LeClair have learned so quickly of Travis's whereabouts that night?

Both things, Travis had been quick to point out, could be made to work against the man and would facilitate Travis's plan. "Look," Travis had told his superior later as they'd gone over that day's events, "it's too good a shot to pass up.

Technically, I'm still on medical leave—nobody will think twice if you spread around that you're easing me out because I'm unstable. It's perfectly believable, given Joel's death and my getting shot, and then this episode in Seattle. Whoever tipped off LeClair about my location is sure to pass the word of my forced retirement along, so when I let it be known I'm willing to give LeClair the diamonds—for a little donation to my retirement fund—the bastard's already gonna be primed to buy it.''

Mac had given a low whistle. "I don't know, boyo," he'd said dubiously. "You'd be walking a mighty fine line.''

Travis had shaken his head. "Not if you, me and LeClair are the only ones in on it. I don't even have to meet with the creep—I'll just string him along until you can come up with something we can use to nail his hide to the wall." He'd looked Mac straight in the eye and uttered his first real lie. "I'm not planning to take him out—I'll just keep him hanging on long enough for you to come up with something, anything to nail him with."

Mac had cocked his head to one side and his eyes had started to glitter. "You know," he said finally, "it might just work. I heard through the grapevine that Internal Revenue is interested in our boy." He'd clapped an arm around Travis's shoulder, the beginning of a smile on his usually dour face. "Now, if we go ahead and prosecute LeClair's errand boys for their attempt to murder you, they may get scared and cough up their boss. But if they don't, with an IRS indictment, we could still put that slime away."

And if not? Travis asked himself now, as he had countless times in the intervening days. If it looked like the man who'd ordered Joel's murder might not be brought to justice? Or at least not in the way he deserved? What then?

Then, Travis would do whatever it took to see that LeClair paid.

Except at the moment, with the unrelenting ache in his head and this uncharacteristic lethargy sapping his strength, he'd be hard pressed to manage anything.

Cursing under his breath, he wondered once more what was wrong with him. He didn't remember feeling this awful even after he'd been shot. Then there'd been pain, but not this debilitating weakness.

Maybe it was the ventilation system. Or perhaps he was airsick. That was a thought. If he was experiencing motion sickness, then once on the ground he should feel okay.

He'd better. He was about to embark on a little game of cat and mouse, and he had to be ready for anything. Only Mac, who was scheduled to fly to the Cayman Islands with an agent from the IRS in an attempt to locate LeClair's former accountant, knew Travis was actually going to be in Seattle to negotiate the "return" of the jewels to LeClair.

It should be more a test of wills than a matter of danger; all he had to do was lie low and let LeClair do the worrying. Even so, a cool head and steady nerves were going to prove essential. He simply couldn't afford to be sick.

Unfortunately his body didn't seem to agree. By the time they'd landed and it was time to disembark, it took his full concentration simply to stand upright, and it was all he could do to follow the other passengers across the satellite terminal and onto the underground train to the main terminal. When he reached the main concourse and the escalator that would take him to the baggage-claim area, the persistent pain in the back of his head had increased to the point where he had to stop and lean against a pillar for support. Nausea rolled through him, nearly bringing him to his knees.

A little way down the corridor, the men's room beckoned like an oasis. God, if he could just make it there. Clenching his jaw, he set out, the door wavering before his gaze. Finally he reached his goal. He pushed open the door and headed for the sinks, hoping that a splash of cold water would clear his head and restore at least some of his strength.

He didn't realize he was not alone, until a scruffy young man appeared in front of him, blocking his path.

"Hey, man, you okay?" he asked, as Travis tried to push past him.

Travis shook his head, trying to clear it. Alarm bells were going off; instinct warned he was in serious trouble here.

"Man, he looks bad," a second juvenile remarked, as Travis clutched the sink for support.

"You can say that again," Travis muttered as the room whirled out from under his feet and he began a slow slide to the floor.

He could hear the two young men talking, discussing his collapse, but he couldn't seem to make sense out of what they were saying. He tried to sit up, but his body wouldn't obey.

Then someone leaned down and rolled him onto his side, riffling for his wallet. His coat was opened, the folder holding his return ticket and the claim checks for his luggage removed from his inside pocket. Travis tried to grab his attacker, but his hand was easily knocked away.

He fell back, smacking his head on the cold tile floor. The room spun, and what followed seemed to be happening to someone else. He was vaguely aware of an exclamation of concern, and then a small hoard of men crowded around him. Next came a parade of uniforms. There was an older man with a badge proclaiming he was from airport security, then a younger man who was obviously with the police. Next came two blue-clad paramedics who quickly checked him over before placing him on a gurney.

And then everything began to spin, and he found himself remembering another time, a crazy ride and a blonde with forever eyes.... And then he remembered nothing.

Four

————

When he awoke, Alex was bending over him.

At first, Travis thought it was another dream. He'd been thinking about her on the plane, and now here she was, standing so close, a fluffy pink cashmere sweater clinging to her soft curves, her glossy hair in a loose braid trailing over her shoulder. "Hi," she said softly.

He raised his hand, thinking to grasp that long, golden braid and tug her closer, but the sight of his own bare arm stopped him cold. He glanced down, staring in bemusement at the patterned blue-and-white cotton draping his chest. "What the hell?" He struggled to sit up.

"Easy," Alex cautioned, curling a hand around his shoulder and firmly but gently pushing him back down.

He took a look around at the cloth-draped walls, the portable monitors crowding the small space, and took a deep breath, registering the distinctive aroma of disinfectant. There was no question about it; this was no dream.

That particular scent was the same whether you were in an infirmary in Senegal or a clinic in Greenland. He was in the hospital.

He jumped to the most obvious conclusion. "Have I been shot again?"

Horror bloomed in Alex's dark brown eyes. "Again?" she echoed faintly. "No, of course not."

Ignoring her stricken look, he took stock, starting with his toes and carefully working his way up. "You're right," he said finally. As a matter of fact, the only things wrong with him seemed to be a vicious headache and the same general weakness that had done him in at the airport.

Airport? He had a sudden blurry memory of a pair of punks standing over him, of hands searching feverishly through his clothes. "Sonofabitch," he muttered darkly, chagrined as he realized he'd been rolled by a pair of post-pubescent hoodlums. Even as a wave of embarrassment flushed his skin, his eyes narrowed on Alex as it occurred to him to wonder what she was doing here. Every time he had a problem, it seemed she was close at hand. "What day is it, anyway?" he asked, irritably, impatient with his own un-accustomed grogginess. "And what are you doing here?"

Alex blinked at the hostility in his voice, but her composure didn't waver. "It's Saturday. You were brought in early this morning. The hospital called me at 7 a.m. They found my card in your pocket and asked me to come, hoping I could identify you." Her soft voice turned gently chiding. "You didn't have any other identification. You really should be more careful, especially in your line of work. What if you hadn't had my card and you really had been shot? Nobody would have had the slightest idea who you are, and you wouldn't have been able to tell them."

He glared at her, only to quickly discover that scrunching up his eyes accelerated the pounding in his head.

"Look," he said gruffly, "I did have ID, okay? Somebody must have stolen my wallet...after I passed out." Why was he lying? Why didn't he want her to know he'd been so weak he'd been as easy to overpower as an infant? What the hell did he care what she thought?

"That's terrible." Her hand automatically covered his, giving it a compassionate squeeze.

That was why. She was just too damn...physical, and the last thing on earth he wanted was her sympathy. Sliding his hand away, ostensibly to drag the sheet that covered him to the waist higher, he asked, "So if I wasn't shot, what the hell's wrong with me?"

Silence. Glancing up, Travis realized that for the first time since he'd met her, Alex looked distinctly uncomfortable. Alarm bells went off in his head. He jerked upright, ignoring the pain that zinged through his head. "What is it?" he demanded, beating back the panic trying to sneak up on him. Was it really serious? Could it be something terminal?

Naw, it couldn't be. Like he'd told Alex just two weeks ago, he was in great shape. He ought to be. He'd worked like a demon to get back in shape after the shooting, pushing himself relentlessly. Now he ran at least five miles three times a week and there was enough manual labor on his farm, feeding the horses and cows and goats, cleaning stalls, repairing fences and the like, to keep him in more than adequate physical shape.

Besides, if he was terminally ill, wouldn't he have had some advance warning? You didn't just wake up one morning at the prime age of thirty-four and keel over dead from a headache. Did you?

He sat up even straighter and was immediately assaulted by another wave of dizziness. Maybe he was sicker than he thought. "What is it? Tell me what the hell they think's the matter."

"I...it's—"

"Chicken pox, Mr. Cross." A tired-looking young resident wearing standard hospital greens pulled back the curtain and stepped inside. He shot Alex an appreciative glance, looked down at Travis's chart, then snatched a sterile thermometer off the bedside stand, tore off the wrapping, shook it down and stuffed it into Travis's surprised mouth. "At least, that's our best educated guess. I'm Dr. Schadelman, by the way. According to Ms. Wright, you're perfectly on schedule if you were exposed fifteen days ago." Making a note in the chart he held in his hand, he missed the startled look Travis shot Alex and her apologetic response. "Have you been feeling fatigued?" the doctor asked. At Travis's curt nod he scribbled briefly. "Headache?" Another nod, another scribble. "Umm-hmm. Let's take a look at you then."

Setting down the chart, he stepped forward and whipped the sheet down and the hospital gown up, examining Travis's torso and underarm area, palpitating his flat, hard abdomen, pressing with deft fingers in the area of kidneys, appendix and spleen. "Umm-hmm," he murmured. Tenting the sheet so Travis's lower body was shielded from Alex, he continued the examination. "How long since you sustained the injury to your thigh?"

The two men's eyes met. "Five months," Travis replied.

The doctor nodded. "Fast healer. Military? Or law enforcement?" Although the resident's tone was casual, his gaze was intent.

Aware that Alex was soaking up every word, Travis said mildly, "Government service—but I've retired. Now, I'm just a Connecticut farmer." The key to any good cover was consistency.

Dr. Schadelman dropped the sheet. "Great pecs, by the way." He smiled self-deprecatingly. "Every free moment I have I spend either studying or sleeping. My girlfriend says I have the muscle tone of a marshmallow,'' he confided as he took Travis's chin in his hands and gently rotated Travis's head. He proceeded to peer behind his patient's ears, then examined his scalp. Finally Dr. Schadelman pulled the thermometer loose, glanced at it, said "umm-hmm," several times more and wrote again in the chart.

He looked up. "Yep, it's chicken pox," he said cheerfully. "You've got all the symptoms—a fever of a hundred and one, you're feeling tired, and you've got a headache. You've also got several large areas of skin covered with flat, reddish splotches, and you already have some raised pimples and even a few vesicles. Judging by the extent of those blotchy areas, I'd say you're in for a pretty tough time of it. Good thing you have Ms. Wright here to take care of you.''

Resisting the urge to leap off the bed and strangle the depressingly healthy-looking young doctor, Travis said carefully, "Let's get a few things straight, *Doctor*. First, I do not have chicken pox. I had it when I was five. I remember distinctly—the glands in my neck were so swollen I looked like an overly ambitious chipmunk.''

"Well, that explains it then," Dr. Schadelman said blithely.

He was so cheerful Travis knew it wasn't good news. "Explains what?" he demanded.

"What you're describing, Mr. Cross," the doctor said benevolently, "isn't chicken pox. What you had was the mumps.''

"I'm telling you," Travis said stubbornly, "I do not have chicken pox. I *refuse* to have chicken pox. Although—" his gaze swung to Alex "—I can't wait to hear just where Ms. Wright fits into this.''

"It was Brandon," she answered quickly, her clear brown eyes asking his forgiveness. "He was infectious the night of my party."

Travis digested that little piece of news. "But since I don't have chicken pox," he said with unimpeachable logic, "it can't be his fault." He turned to the doctor, effectively dismissing her, and added coolly, "Nor do I need Ms. Wright's help. I can take care of myself. Now, I want to see a real doctor. Somebody who looks like Marcus Welby instead of Doogie Howser."

"My, my, my." Dr. Schadelman appeared completely undaunted. "I can see Ms. Wright wasn't exaggerating when she mentioned you tend to be a little cranky when you don't get your own way."

"I am not cranky," Travis said between gritted teeth, forgetting his aching head long enough to send Alex a fulminating glance.

Dr. Schadelman gave a rude snort. "Right. Well, I'll be happy to get another doctor for a second opinion, but while I'm gone, I suggest you reconsider your options. Ms. Wright has volunteered to pay your bill and take you home with her, which isn't a bad offer." He beamed at Alex, his eyes warm as they trailed from her soft pink sweater to the pair of stone-washed jeans hugging her slim hips and long legs. "I'd go if she asked me."

"Well, she didn't," Travis snapped.

Dr. Schadelman gave a sigh. "I'll go find someone for your second opinion, but I strongly suggest you think about what I said. I can't imagine you're feeling very well, and it's going to get worse before it gets better." He bustled out.

In point of truth, Travis *wasn't* feeling too good. The skin on his face and neck was beginning to burn, his headache showed no signs of relenting, and he felt like he could sleep for a week. Which he would do, he promised himself, just as soon as he got rid of Alex. "Look," he said in a tone he meant to sound conciliatory, "I don't mean to seem ungrateful, but I can take care of myself. I mean, well, hell, I've been on my own for years—I'm used to being alone."

Alex crossed her arms over her breasts. "Yes? Well, that's very admirable, I'm sure, but just where do you plan to go to be on your own?"

"A hotel, of course." Travis rubbed a weary hand across his forehead.

"And just how do you propose to pay for this hotel?"

"I..." Hell, he hadn't thought about that. Damn those two punks!

"Given," Alex persisted, "that you can even get a hotel to take you in. I can't imagine anyone eager to register a guest who can't walk without falling down and whose face is looking more and more like dotted swiss with every passing minute. Of course, once you explain you have no luggage, no identification, no credit cards and no money, and that you'll only be infectious for a week or so, I'm sure they'll welcome you with open arms."

He was going to throttle her just as soon as he had the energy. "Are you done?"

"Have you given up this crazy obsession with self-sufficiency? I agree it's an admirable trait, but frankly, you're carrying it to outlandish heights. You're also wasting a huge chunk of my Saturday, which for myself I wouldn't mind, but my neighbor Connie drove me here in her van because the Ferrari is in the shop, so you're not simply inconveniencing me with your pigheadedness, but somebody else, too."

"Listen, lady," he shot back, coming bolt upright, "I wasn't the one who called you. I told you you can go—so go already!" The room was starting to do the familiar spin he recognized from the airport.

Alex raised her hands in a gesture of surrender. "Okay, fine," she said, picking up her navy suede jacket from the chair.

Travis sagged back against the pillows, staring at her suspiciously. "What do you mean, 'Fine?'"

She shrugged into her coat. "You want me to go, I'm going."

"Yeah?" She was really going? Just like that? "Well. Great."

"See you around, Cross." Before he had a chance to formulate a reply, she parted the curtains and was gone.

Travis couldn't believe it. All he'd had to do was ask and she'd gone. She'd actually *left,* the only evidence she'd even been there the faintest lingering trace of her perfume.

So why wasn't he feeling deliriously happy? Why, in point of fact, did he feel . . . abandoned?

It had nothing to do with Alexis Wright, he told himself hastily. He didn't need her; what he needed was a phone. All he had to do was call Mac, and Mac would take care of everything.

Unless Mac was already on his way to the Caymans.

He wasn't even going to consider that. Looking around the small cubicle, he spotted his clothes in the corner, neatly folded and stacked. Okay. He'd just get dressed, find the nearest pay phone, call Mac, and he'd be out of here. Gritting his teeth, he swung his legs over the edge of the bed and reached for his pants.

Standing unobtrusively down the hall, Alex leaned back against the wall, glancing from her watch to Travis's cubicle. All she could see beneath the curtains were his feet, but it was enough. A slight smile curved her lips as she watched him try for the third time to get his jeans on. He was about as light on his feet as a water buffalo.

Spotting Dr. Schadelman farther down the hallway, she waved and took a sip of coffee from the paper cup in her hand, grimacing at the bitter taste of the stuff while hoping it would drown the butterflies zooming around in her stomach.

What was she doing here, anyway? And with a man who'd recently been shot, for heaven's sake! She was still reeling both from that little piece of information and the unemotional way he'd revealed it, as if it was of no more import than a mosquito bite.

But then, in his world, it probably wasn't.

His *former* world, she reminded herself, immediately feeling better. Still, what was she thinking, offering to take in a man who was, for all practical purposes, a stranger? All she knew about him was that up until recently he'd been some sort of government agent and that she was responsible, however unwittingly, for his present case of chicken pox.

He was also one terrific kisser.

Which had nothing to do with anything, she told herself sternly. Determined to ignore that treacherous train of thought, she took her first good look at her surroundings and saw the doctors and nurses bustling around.

She wrinkled her nose against the odor of antiseptic. Up until now, she'd been so concerned about Travis she'd nearly forgotten how much she hated hospitals. She frowned, trying to remember the last time she'd been in one. When Lizabeth and Brandon were born? No. Sarah had been home so fast both times she hadn't had to come.

Then when? It had to have been ... The familiar sense of panic came flooding back as she was slammed by an avalanche of remembered loss.

Oh, Lord. How could she have forgotten? It had to have been when Stefan ... A tremor shuddered through her. She drew a deep breath and forced herself to relax before it could get out of hand.

She could handle this. So okay, she hadn't been in a hospital since Stefan was killed. But nobody was dying now, and the only reason she was here was that Travis Cross didn't have anyone else. It was hardly as if she cared for him; she was simply doing him a slight favor. She would see to his immediate needs until he could get a hold of a friend, and then he would be on his way again.

With that settled to her satisfaction, she leaned back against the wall to wait. She'd give him five minutes, she decided. If he was still fumbling around then, she'd...what? Leave without him? Or go help him get his pants on? She could just imagine Mr. Independence's reaction to *that*.

Luckily she didn't have to decide. Exactly four and a half minutes later, Travis came stumbling through the curtains. He was a sight to behold. He had his shirt on, but it was unbuttoned and untucked. He had his jeans on, and they were zipped if not snapped. He was barefoot. His hair was standing on end. And as if he needed the weight for balance, he had his cowboy boots clutched in one upraised hand, his leather bomber jacket held high in the other.

He looked like an out-of-control high-wire act.

Alex stared, her coffee cup frozen halfway to her mouth. Dr. Schadelman was right. The man did have great pecs. And great deltoids, and...how was it the sight of his exposed navel had the power to make her think highly erotic, decidedly libidinous thoughts?

She was a mature adult. She didn't usually react this way to men. She didn't usually react *any* way to men. Or at least she hadn't until she met Travis Cross—and seen his killer navel.

Shaking her head at her own folly, she watched as Travis, who was so intent on putting one foot in front of the other he didn't even see her standing there, lurched past, clearly headed toward the bank of pay phones opposite the nurses' station. Patiently she sipped the lukewarm coffee, steeling herself against the urge to run to his aid as he pitched into the wall several times before finally reaching his destination.

Tossing his boots and jacket to the floor, Travis yanked the receiver free and held the cool plastic to his forehead as he struggled to remember the SDSS number in Washington, D.C. When it finally came to him, he impatiently placed the call, making it station-to-station collect on the off chance Mac wasn't in.

A woman answered, her voice high, nasal and unfamiliar, but at least she agreed to accept his call. Travis sagged with relief, shifting the receiver closer to his ear and resting his forehead against the enclosure's wall. "Derwin MacGregor," he said hoarsely.

"I'm sorry, sir," came that tinny, impersonal voice. "Mr. MacGregor is unavailable at this time."

Hell. "He'll be available to me. Tell him it's Travis Cross calling."

"I've already noted your name, sir. I'm sorry, but Mr. MacGregor is not in the office."

Travis's grip tightened on the receiver. *Damn it, Mac was already gone.* He took a deep breath and tried to think. "Then let me talk to Stella, his secretary, please." Stella would vouch for him. Actually, she would be better than Mac. She'd been with the Department for longer than anyone could remember and was the most efficient person Travis had ever met. She practically ran the place.

"I'm sorry, sir. Ms. Walford is unavailable."

Travis's temper snapped. "Well, where the hell is she? When will she be back?"

"I'm sorry, sir. Ms. Walford will not be available until the first."

"The first of what, for heaven's sake?" She couldn't mean the first of May, could she? That was—holy hell, that was nearly two weeks away! Taking several deep breaths in order to calm himself, he said reasonably enough, "Okay, okay. Then can you at least get a message to Mac for me?"

Did the tinny voice on the other end of the line seem to be sounding more and more smug each time she thwarted him? Or was he losing it? "I'm sorry, sir. The Department doesn't handle messages from unauthorized personnel."

She definitely sounded smug. "I *am* authorized, you—" He took another deep breath. He was definitely losing it. Screaming at a faceless voice three thousand miles away wasn't going to accomplish anything. "My employee number is 55-592-7614H."

"One moment, pleeze."

This was not happening to him. It was all a bad dream; he was still on the plane. Any minute now the stewardess would wake him up to tell him they were landing. He'd feel great. One way or another, in the next few days LeClair would get what he had coming to him, and in no time Travis would be on his way to his next assignment.

"Excuse me, sir?"

"What?"

"I'm sorry, sir, but our records list you as on inactive status. Your identification has expired."

"Yes, I know, but—"

"I'm sorry, sir. Government regulations prohibit me from accepting collect calls from inactives. Good day, sir."

"No! Don't hang—" The line went dead in his ear.

He looked up. Alex was standing there, his boots and coat in her hand. Flanking her was Dr. Schadelman and an older man. The older man stepped forward and without a word, took a closer look at the rash that by then had spread from behind Travis's ears down his neck, and from beneath his arms to his ribs.

"Don't tell me," Travis said tiredly. "I know. It's—"

"Chicken pox," the older doctor said. His tone brooked no contradiction.

Travis's gaze swung to Alex. "I've paid the bill," she informed him.

There was no use pretending any longer. The damn hallway was starting to tilt, just like the airport terminal had done. If he didn't do something soon, he'd be meeting the linoleum nose first.

Clutching the telephone for balance, he scowled at Alex. "You promise you're not driving?"

"Cross my heart," she said, in her soft, sincere voice.

Well, hell. How the heck could a fellow doubt her when she put it like that? He sighed and relinquished the phone. "Okay. Let's go."

Connie's driving mirrored her looks; it, too, was cautious and conservative. Out of the corner of her eye, Alex watched as Travis absorbed this fact over the course of several blocks. She couldn't contain a small smile when he finally settled back against the car seat, gave an audible sigh of relief and fell quickly to sleep.

A peaceful silence descended, broken only by the even rhythm of Travis's breathing and the low-pitched hum of the van's engine as they headed out of Seattle across the Evergreen Point Floating Bridge. Alex stared at the broad expanse of Lake Washington sparkling in the mild April sunshine. Sailboats by the score skimmed across the lake's indigo surface. To the southeast, Mount Rainier rose like a giant, inverted ice-cream cone, back-dropped in azure and frosted with snow.

Yet Alex was blind to the beauty of the golden spring day, her thoughts directed inwardly as she continued to wonder if she was doing the right thing.

But what else could she have done? Leave a sick man to cope alone? It wasn't as if he had someone he could depend on. She knew that from his curt no when she'd asked him if there was someone else he wanted to call after he'd made his single, apparently very frustrating phone call. Something in his eyes when he'd replied in the negative had hinted at a terrible alienation, suggesting a man who expected to be left to manage alone. What would it be like not to have anyone to depend on, to trust?

Alex, who had a community of friends who loved her, who shared and enriched her life, couldn't imagine that. But she knew deep down it was part of the reason she was taking Travis home with her. She just couldn't stand the thought of anyone being so terribly alone.

Not, she thought wryly, that he would thank her for such maudlin reasoning. He kept his tender emotions more closely guarded than the gold at Fort Knox. He was stubborn, independent—and determined to keep his distance.

Which was okay with her. She certainly wasn't looking for an involvement; she was just being a good Samaritan. It had nothing, she told herself sternly, to do with the fact that the one kiss they'd shared had been incendiary enough to set her ablaze like a tinder-dry forest on a hot summer's day.

It wasn't as if she'd never been kissed before, she thought, fidgeting in her seat. She'd be the first to admit that she didn't have the experience of someone like DeeDee, but she'd had her share of teenage romances, and she had, after all, been married. She was past the point in her life where basic animal magnetism meant more to her than personality.

Wasn't she?

Deciding to put the matter to the test, she dragged her gaze from Mount Rainier and shifted around to check on the focus of her thoughts, who was fast asleep on the van's back bench seat.

She knew the instant her gaze rested on Travis's unguarded face that she'd made a big mistake. He slept with the innocent abandon of a little boy, his legs outstretched and his arms flung out. With his hair rumpled, the buttons on his rust-brown shirt mismatched, and all the lines of tension smoothed from his face, he seemed absurdly young and vulnerable.

Just looking at him made Alex ache with an urge to protect him while at the same time her fingers tingled with the need to touch him. So much for the character-versus-charisma theory; apparently she wasn't quite as immune to his particular brand of appeal as she'd thought.

Which didn't mean she had to succumb to it, she told herself, swiveling forward decisively to gaze unseeingly once more at the passing scenery. Nor did she have to like it. Her life was *settled*. She had her home, her job, her friends. She didn't need some handsome stranger with a self-sufficiency complex confusing things.

Did she?

She gave a heartfelt sigh of relief when they pulled into her driveway, eager for some physical activity as a refuge from her thoughts. The van had barely rolled to a halt before she had her door open and was climbing out.

Almost immediately, Sarah, with Brandon bounding after her, came hurrying out of Alex's house.

"Is he here? Huh? Huh? Is Travis here?" Brandon exclaimed excitedly, dancing around Alex to get a look inside the van. Scooting past his mother and Alex, he leaned into the van and stared at the man asleep on the seat. He frowned. "What did you do to him, Auntie Alex?"

"Hush," Sarah said, drawing her son back from the open door and giving Alex and apologetic look. "Alex didn't do anything to him. He's just sick. You remember how you felt when you had the chicken pox?" He nodded, and she went on. "Well, that's the way he feels."

"Oh," Brandon said. The minute she turned to talk to Alex and Connie, he wiggled free of her grasp and climbed into the van to get a closer look at Travis, who promptly opened one bleary eye and stared back.

"He's awake!" Brandon chimed, jumping up and down, rocking the van.

The motion brought a heartfelt groan from Travis. He pressed a hand to eyes. "Hey, buddy," he muttered.

"Brandon, get down from there," Sarah instructed, grabbing her son's arm and pulling him out of the van so Alex could lean in.

"We're here," she stated unnecessarily, sliding the door of the van completely open.

Travis's arm lifted. His eyes were glazed with fever, and he shivered involuntarily at the slight April breeze drifting in the open door. It seemed to take him a moment to figure out where "here" was.

"You'll feel better once we get you into the house," Alex said. As if doubting her words, he rolled his head to stare through the van window at the house, its white paint gleaming in the bright spring sunshine.

He leaned back and let his eyes drift shut again. "Just leave me alone and let me die in peace," he grumbled. Alex felt a pang of sympathy; he looked as wrung out as yesterday's wash.

"Is Travis going to live with Alex now, Mommy?" Brandon inquired, watching Alex help Travis from the van. The child's question halted the two adults in question in midstride.

"Ah, no," Sarah choked out. "He's just going to stay with her for a while, because he's sick."

Alex steadied Travis as he stepped down from the van. "Come on," she said softly to him. "Let's get you into the house."

She slid her arm around him only to have him immediately sidle away. "I can make it myself," he said gruffly. Suiting actions to words, he started doggedly up the walk and slowly climbed the steps. When he reached the screen door and she was still standing where he'd left her, he cast her an impatient glance. "Well?" One brow rose sardonically, the effect only slightly nullified by the puffiness of his face.

Already stung by his pointed rejection, his sarcasm was enough to galvanize Alex into action. She marched to his side, flung open the door and ushered him in. Very aware of his tall, brooding presence behind her, she led the way upstairs.

Originally, the old farmhouse had boasted six bedrooms on the second floor, three on either side of the stairs. The only bathroom in the house had been downstairs off the kitchen. Since Alex had wanted the convenience of upstairs plumbing, she'd had the second floor extensively remodeled. The two far bedrooms had been made into a master bedroom that straddled the width of the house, with its own bath in half of what had been the left middle bedroom. The other half of the former left middle bedroom was now a guest bathroom, and the near left bedroom, which was quite small, she used for storage.

The remaining two rooms on the right had been combined to make a single large guest room, and it was there she took Travis. It was a pleasant room, light and airy, with windows facing both north and east, thick, cream-colored carpet on the floor, and simple, pale-oak furniture. The bedspread and curtains were a mix of blue, beige and cream in a subdued geometric pattern. On one side of the bed was an old bentwood rocker that had been her grandmother's, and on the other was a nightstand with a squat brass lamp and blue slimline phone. A blue-and-white quilt Alex had made herself was draped on the end of the bed.

"Here we are," she said, smoothing the already wrinkle-free quilt with her hand. She was, she realized abruptly, nervous. Which was ridiculous. What on earth did she have to be nervous about? It wasn't as if she'd never been in a bedroom with a man before. Why, at the height of the re-modeling, she'd been in this very room with several different men.

Of course they'd all been workmen, and none of them had the effect on her that Travis did, which, she acknowledged ruefully, was a sort of hormonal call of the wild. Still, she ought to be able to conduct herself with a modicum of dignity.

She turned toward the object of her thoughts, who was standing in the doorway, leaning tiredly against the jamb, and the sight of him, big, solid and real, unnerved her even more. She was so discomfited, she blurted out the first thing that came to mind. "Why don't you get undressed?"

He straightened instantly, giving her a narrow look. "Why?" he asked suspiciously.

Alex wondered what his reaction would be if she said, *So I can have my wild and wicked way with you.* Stifling the urge to find out, she moved around to the head of the bed and began to turn down the spread, telling herself to get serious. In what she hoped was a steady voice, she said, "So you can get into bed while I call the pharmacy to see if the prescription Dr. Schadelman was going to call in for you is ready." She gave him what she hoped was a nonthreatening smile.

His scowl deepened, but after a second he moved farther into the room and sat down gingerly on the edge of the bed. "Okay." He crossed one foot over the knee of the opposite outstretched leg, effectively trapping her by the headboard while he tugged off first one boot and then the other.

Alex stared at his feet, remembering how he'd looked in the hospital, barefoot *and* bare-naveled. "What happened to your socks?" Even to her own ears, her voice sounded husky and strained.

Travis glanced at her briefly, but if he noted her uneasiness, it didn't show. He stood, took off his leather jacket, tossed it on the rocker and shrugged. "I don't know. I couldn't find them at the hospital." He pulled the top button of his shirt free. Then his hand moved lower, to the next button. And the next.

And the next thing *Alex* knew, she was staring at his broad bare chest, with its narrow wedge of dark silk curls, transfixed as his hand hovered over the closure of his jeans. In the sudden silence, the soft pop when he unsnapped them seemed to reverberate like a cannon shot.

Alex shuddered. Why did the room seem to be shrinking along with his attire? Why was she suddenly so warm? Maybe *she* was getting a fever.

One thing was for sure. She had to get out of here before Travis realized he could make her hyperventilate merely by removing his shirt.

"I'll just go make that call," she said, inadvertently brushing the soft skin of her wrist against his muscled forearm as she sidled past him toward the door.

"Right." Travis didn't even look up.

Clutching her traitorously tingling arm, Alex fled.

Five

Travis Cross slept in his briefs.

Alex stood in her kitchen, staring blindly at the loaded tray sitting on the counter as tantalizing images of Travis in his underwear stole into her mind. No boxer shorts for Mr. Cross. Oh, no. He wore black briefs, blue briefs, and since he didn't suffer a major fixation with modesty, she knew they were... brief briefs.

It was because his luggage had yet to be recovered that Alex was on such intimate terms with Travis's underwear. Since Travis was in no shape to shop for himself, she'd been given the dubious pleasure of doing it for him. She now knew he wore jeans with a thirty-four-inch inseam, size twelve sneakers and preferred crew-neck T-shirts, again in navy or black. And, as noted, no pajamas at all.

Why did she continue to feel a slight thrill over that last fact? Maybe the girls were right. Maybe she'd been so long without a man she was going over the edge. Maybe...

She gave herself a shake. She was *not* going to think about that. Straightening her shoulders, she gave the legs of her modest khaki shorts a tug, straightened the collar of her pale yellow blouse, then smoothed back her hair in its demure French braid. Forcing her attention back to the tray, she reviewed its contents, running through a mental checklist.

Clean place mat, two napkins, silverware, *check.* Chicken noodle soup, more noodles than broth, served in a mug—according to a certain person, it cooled too rapidly in a bowl—*check*. Raspberry jello cut into precise one-inch squares, an even dozen saltine crackers and a 7-Up on ice in a tall, not a short, glass. *Check.*

She reminded herself, as she had about a hundred times in the past six days, of the need to be patient. After all, she'd asked for this. Of course, said a traitorous little voice in her head, that was before she'd known that Mr. SDSS—which definitely did *not* stand for So Darned Self-Sufficient—would settle in and discover he enjoyed being waited on with the zeal of a Third World potentate.

She picked up the tray, then, frowning, set it down again and mutinously added the small bottle of medicine Dr. Schadelman had prescribed. She headed for the stairs.

Travis greeted her arrival suspiciously. "Is that chicken noodle?"

Alex gave him a sweet smile. "Uh-huh. There's no need to beat *me* over the head with a stick. I learned my lesson about trying to broaden your culinary horizons when I caught you pouring the minestrone on my dieffenbachia. Now, where would you like this?" *On your head?*

As if he'd heard that last comment, he gave her a guarded look, quickly took the tray and settled it on his lap. "Hey— I told you all I wanted was chicken noodle. It's a proven fact chicken soup has actual medicinal value. But minestrone?"

He gave a little shudder. "I wouldn't wish minestrone on anything—animal, mineral or vegetable."

"Great," Alex murmured to herself, "all about soup from a nut." She sat down in her grandmother's rocker to keep him company while he ate—the routine they'd settled into over the past few days. Leaning down, she pulled the muffler she'd started from her knitting bag. "At least the minestrone was homemade. Do you know how much sodium is in canned soup?" She picked up her knitting needles and cast on.

"No," Travis said, the picture of bliss as he swallowed a spoonful of broth, "but I have this bad feeling you're about to tell me."

"Trust me, you don't want to know," she responded repressively.

He crumbled crackers in his fist and dropped them into the mug. "Hey, look, I only drink in moderation, I don't smoke, and I don't play around, so just leave my soup alone."

Alex wisely didn't respond. Instead, she focused on her hands and tried to concentrate on knitting, refusing to analyze whether the slight pang she felt at Travis's contention he didn't play around was relief or disappointment. When he was done, she laid the yarn and needles aside, took the tray from him and set it on the floor. With an inner sigh, she picked up the untouched bottle of medicine and the spoon, and straightened.

Instantly Travis's expression grew truculent. He crossed his arms over his chest, which was—Alex noted thankfully—covered in a black T-shirt. "You might as well put it away."

Although Alex's calm facade didn't falter, she wished she had the courage to rap him right between the eyes with the spoon. "Why are you being so stubborn?" she asked, telling herself not to lose sight of the bright side in this. At least the horrible case of chicken pox Dr. Schadelman had predicted had never materialized. While Travis might feel lower than a snake in a gully, his rash was relatively mild. Already, most of his pox were scabbed over.

Still, he itched, and judging from the way he'd been squirming all through the meal, it was getting worse. And still he flatly refused to take the antihistamine the "kid" doctor had prescribed to relieve his itching. "I don't get it," she said softly as he scratched furiously behind his left ear. "You don't strike me as a masochist."

Travis decided that was debatable as his hooded gaze slid over her long, bare legs and he rejected the urge to haul her into bed with him. He knew she wasn't doing it on purpose, but her soft voice and gentle hands and velvety skin were driving him crazy.

He wanted to touch her, damn it. He wanted to slide his hands up under the bottom of her shorts and stroke her smooth, supple thighs, he wanted to press his mouth to the hollow of her throat and taste the flavor of her pale, golden skin, he wanted to nuzzle her breasts and shape her nipples with his lips.

There wasn't a medicine in the world that was going to relieve that particular itch, although for a minute he was tempted to try. Then reason reasserted itself, along with years and years of habit. Drugs—of any kind—were dangerous. They muddled your brain and blunted your reactions and he wasn't taking any. Period. "I'm not a masochist," he said firmly. "I just make it a rule never to touch anything reputed to taste like bubblegum." He scratched furiously at his chest.

Alex studied him. "Sarah swears Brandon liked it when he was sick."

"What do you expect," Travis grumbled, "from someone who cheats at checkers and claims his favorite food is something called Nerds? What the hell are Nerds?"

Since it didn't appear he was going to take his medicine, Alex set it on the tray and picked up her knitting. "Nerds are itsy-bitsy neon-colored candies that come in flavors like guava, banana and passion fruit. Kids drop them on your carpet and they ruin your vacuum cleaner."

Despite himself, Travis's mouth curved at her explanation. "About what I'd expect from Brandon."

Alex smiled in return. "Nerds aren't any worse than some of the stuff we liked as kids. Remember Pixy Stix?"

"Pixiestixs?" Travis looked blank. "No."

Alex looked at him curiously. "Don't you remember? They were big about the time we were in grade school. A sour powder in long, thin paper tubes? You tap the stuff out of the tube and onto your tongue."

Travis gave her a disparaging look. "Lady, I spent my grade-school years at a military school, and believe me, there was nothing remotely approaching what you're describing in the St. Alban's commissary."

Alex wasn't sure what to say. Up till now, he'd been pretty closedmouthed about his past; the fact he was volunteering information was unusual. Intrigued, but afraid if she appeared to be prying he'd clam up, she kept her tone light. "Ah. So that's where you learned to bite the bullet. No Pixy Stix."

For just a second he looked startled. Then something that could have been appreciation lit his eyes. "Yeah. Something like that."

With a slight sense of shock, Alex realized they were actually conversing, a first for the week. Maybe, with a little luck, she was finally going to get a few answers to go with her many questions. "Were you there long?" she asked in a casual tone, deciding to start small and work up to the big questions.

"At St. Alban's? Eight years. My mother's second husband thought I was in need of a little discipline, so he convinced her to send me there. He was gone by Christmas, but I was there for the duration."

Alex tried to imagine Travis in the strict atmosphere of a military academy. If her own experience was anything to go by, he was not someone for whom following orders came easily. "I bet you were glad to get home."

"I didn't say I went home," he said, his tone offhand.

A little crease appeared between Alex's brows. "Oh. College?"

He shook his head. "Prep school."

"Prep school?" She did a little quick arithmetic in her head, then asked carefully, "Just how old were you when you first went away to school?"

"Five."

She bit back the appalled protest that rose to her lips. Five! Why, that was Brandon's age. What kind of woman sent her *baby* away, for heaven's sake? From a few other things Travis had let drop over the course of the past few days, the picture Alex had formed of his mother wasn't a very complimentary one; the woman had apparently been vain and immature and had married more times than Carter's had pills. But now, as it became obvious Travis's mom had packed her son away like an excess piece of baggage, Alex was swamped with actual dislike. Yet she knew, from Travis's brutally unemotional tone, that he wouldn't welcome any sympathy. So all she said was, "Oh. I see."

There was an awkward little pause before he said abruptly, "My mother was young. My dad died before I was a year old." He gave a dismissive shrug. "I guess I was what you'd call a handful, and she just wasn't up to raising me on her own.''

Alex's empathy for him increased at his willingness to make excuses for a woman who'd so obviously hurt him. Yet at the same time, she wondered if perhaps he didn't still harbor an illusion that there was something wrong with *him* that had caused his mother to send him away. But again, she doubted he'd welcome her views.

Taking refuge in action from her strong desire to air her opinion, she began to gather her needles and yarn into her knitting bag, so she was caught unprepared for Travis's next words. "Hey, look," he said caustically, misreading her agitation, "I don't need your pity, okay?"

Alex jerked, sending the bright blue ball of wool flying, to bounce off his chest. Regaining her composure, she managed to say evenly, "Don't be silly. I just think it's sad your mother didn't have the sense to appreciate what she had."

A flash of surprise blazed briefly in his eyes. He studied her, as if suspecting she might be dissembling, then turned his gaze to the ball of blue yarn, which he picked up. Turning the yarn over and over in his hand, when he finally spoke it was with a calmness that matched her own. "Yeah, well, it really wasn't so bad. She couldn't help who she was, and actually, it helped me later. In my profession, not having close connections is a definite advantage, since it limits the possibility of anyone asking messy questions if you come back from a mission in a body bag."

"But I don't understand," Alex said immediately, suspecting he was trying to shock her but refusing to get sidetracked. "I thought you said you were retired."

"I am," Travis said hastily, then added with forced nonchalance, damning his reckless tongue, "although it'd be more accurate to say I'm in the process. It takes a little time." She was simply too easy to talk to; he kept getting lulled by her soft voice and gentle manner—not to mention those gorgeous legs—into forgetting she had a sharp, inquisitive mind.

Her voice became frankly curious. "So what were you doing the day I met you?"

Travis's mind raced; he had to be careful here. He'd been giving it a lot of thought—hell, he didn't have anything else to do but lie in bed and think—and he'd come to the conclusion that Alex's house was the perfect place to hide out, since there was no knowing when Mac would return to rescue him.

He'd agreed to come to Alex's in the first place only because he'd judged she was in absolutely no danger. But now he was overdue to contact LeClair, and for the past day he'd been trying to calculate whether making a call to the criminal would adversely affect Alex's safety.

He couldn't see that it would. If LeClair tried to track him down, the last place the criminal boss would ever think to look for him was in the oh-so-respectable suburbs, and there was nothing to tie him to Alex.

Still, even though he was absolutely certain there was no danger, he didn't imagine Alex would take kindly to him using her home as his base of operations. People like Alex lived in a sheltered environment, untouched by violence and other unsavory aspects of the world. Probably her only contact with the law had been an occasional traffic ticket. *Occasional? Okay—if the Washington State Patrol was doing its job she ought to have enough citations to wallpaper the mall.* But still. He would be stupid to tell her everything. What if she threw him out?

So why did he still feel reluctant to mislead her? He had deceived a lot of people over the course of his career, and it had never bothered him before. But there was just something about Alex ...

Of course, when he really thought about it, he realized he didn't need to lie, exactly. He couldn't see the harm in telling her *part* of the truth. He just couldn't tell her everything. As for the rest, what she didn't know couldn't hurt her, right?

It wasn't, he consoled himself, as if he had to divulge the President's sock size or tell her any other great state secrets. Besides, in another week he'd be out of here without her ever knowing the difference. "You might as well get comfortable," he said. "If you're going to understand, we need to start at the beginning."

Realizing he'd come to a decision he could live with, he settled more solidly into the pillows. Which was why, when she sat back in the rocker and crossed one slender leg over the other, he wasn't prepared for the heat that seared through him when her shorts crept up on one side. Instantly he found himself imagining what it would feel like if he slipped his hand beneath the fabric and traced the delicate outline of her hipbone with his thumb. He'd spread his fingers wide, and—

"Well?" Alex looked at him quizzically.

His eyes jerked to hers guiltily. "Well what?"

"Are you going to do it or not?"

God, he hoped so. "Do what?"

She frowned, then reached over and pressed her hand to his forehead. "You don't feel hot," she murmured.

Man, was she wrong. He felt like he was going to incinerate, and it didn't help that she was leaning over him, putting him at eye level with the open neckline of her blouse. Her skin looked like satin stretched over her collarbone and her light, floral fragrance filled his nose. His hands clenched into fists as he fought the urge to lock his arms around her and pull her closer so he could sample the warm, creamy skin just inches from his mouth.

Alex moved back. "Travis?" Her confusion grew as she took in the faint flush high on his cheekbones. "What's wrong?"

What's wrong is I'm losing it, he thought in disgust, yanking his gaze from her rounded breasts and willing his racing heart to slow down. What the hell had they been talking about, anyway?

"Are you going to tell me what's going on with you or not?"

That was easy. He was dying—painfully—from unfulfilled lust.

But that wasn't what *Alex* was talking about, and he knew it. He forced himself to concentrate, tearing his mind away from his willful libido and launching into his edited version of the truth. "Two years ago," he began, "the youngest son of one of Europe's oldest royal families was kidnapped while attending school on the East Coast." At her startled look, he added, "It was very hush-hush. There wasn't a word in the papers."

"Ah," Alex said, her expression thoughtful.

"Anyway, State was called in to coordinate efforts between the locals, the FBI and Interpol." He gave one of the dismissive little shrugs she was beginning to recognize as a particular mannerism of his. "The kidnappers demanded three and a half million dollars in first-quality diamonds to release the boy. Although everybody advised against it, the family opted to pay. Thankfully, the victim was recovered unharmed—but the jewels and the crooks disappeared without a trace.

"Then, a little over six months ago, we received a tip. The diamonds were about to be sold by a small-time jeweler named Gordon LeClair. LeClair was a relative unknown—

he'd had a few minor brushes with the law, suspicion of fencing stolen property, that sort of thing, but he'd never been convicted of anything.

"As the agent in charge for State, I assigned a man to investigate him." Not just any man; he'd given his closest friend, Joel Gibson, the task. Although Joel had a reputation for being a little hot-headed, he was also a first-rate investigator. "I thought it was a pretty routine assignment—until my agent called me one night while he was staking out LeClair's shop. He was real excited, claimed he had evidence LeClair was the mastermind behind the kidnapping, and wanted me to come." Travis's eyes darkened. "I got hung up, and by the time I got there, my guy was dead and the evidence had vanished. Then somebody shot me, and by the time I could call for backup, LeClair had disappeared without a trace." Lying helpless in that hospital bed had been the worst experience of his life; he'd been sick with grief and guilt over Joel's unnecessary death, consumed with frustration and fury when no trace of LeClair could be found. That was when he'd made his vow to get the guy; if it took the rest of his life, the bastard was going to pay.

"I was still on medical leave when MacGregor, my boss, called me a few weeks ago. There'd been another tip. The word on the street was that LeClair was in Seattle and the sale of the diamonds was on again. It was set to go down at a little suburban mall."

"My mall?" Alex asked, appalled.

Travis nodded. "Since I knew all the players, Mac felt I was the logical person to represent the Department's interests. Unfortunately things didn't quite go off the way they were supposed to, and I needed a lift. That's where you came in. End of story."

"Wait." Alex's mind raced as her gaze zeroed in on him. "That tells me *why* you were at the mall in the first place, but if I understand this right, the bad guys were supposed to get arrested. Why were they chasing you, instead?" Her big brown eyes were intense.

Travis leaned over and picked his soda up off the tray. He took a long swallow, melted ice and all. "Would you believe good taste?"

"Travis."

"Well, hell," he gave a long-suffering sigh. "I suppose it won't hurt to tell you. See, I was only supposed to be an observer. The feds and the locals were supposed to make the actual arrest, but they never showed. Turns out they, along with my backup, got stuck in traffic on one of the bridges.

"Anyway, I was in the mall, and I saw the buyers arrive, and then two of LeClair's lackeys showed up. I knew they had the diamonds and it was obvious, with nobody there to stop it, the sale was going to go down. So I did the only thing I could—I stole the diamonds."

Alex sucked in a breath. "You what?" she asked on a note of disbelief. "You *stole* them? Why didn't you arrest the crooks?"

Travis gave her a look of ill-concealed impatience. "Because I'm not a cop, Alex. I'm an almost retired State Department agent who has a little place in Connecticut with three goats, a dairy cow and five horses. You'd be surprised how sensitive the local law enforcement gets when out-of-staters start waving guns and making citizen's arrests."

"You have goats?" Try as she might, she couldn't picture remote, enigmatic Travis Cross with goats. Cows or horses, maybe. But goats?

"One of my neighbors gave them to me," he said, running a hand impatiently through his hair. "The point is, I didn't have any authority to make an arrest, and besides, there were way too many civilians around. The idea was to catch these guys during the exchange, not have a shootout with them in the middle of the mall.''

Alex was silent, trying to digest it all. After a few moments, she said, ''So why are you here now?''

He shot her a sour look. ''I have the chicken pox, remember?''

''Not *here* here,'' Alex said patiently, ''but *here.*''

Travis wondered if it should worry him that he understood exactly what she meant. He decided that was probably the least of his problems. ''The two guys I stole the diamonds from—LeClair's henchmen—were the ones chasing me the day we met. That night, after you dropped me off, they were waiting for me at the hotel. They took a few shots at me, but this time my backup was in place, and we caught them cold. They've been charged with attempted murder. The arraignment was supposed to take place yesterday, but because I couldn't make it, it's been postponed until next week.''

''I see,'' Alex said faintly, struggling to conceal her sense of horror. She gave a little shudder. That someone should try to kill Travis was bad enough, but that he should so casually accept the fact chilled her to the bone.

''What?'' Travis demanded, seeing the aversion on her face.

''It's nothing,'' she replied, a little surprised herself at the intensity of her reaction.

He gave a rude snort. ''Give it up, Alex—you're as easy to read as a newspaper headline. I said something wrong.''

She shook her head, watching his long, elegant fingers manipulate the yarn. It was ironic somehow. Hands like his belonged to an artist, not a hired gun. ''No, it's just... I've never understood how anyone can be casual about violence.''

"The world is violent," he said flatly. "You can hide away in your nice little suburb and pretend otherwise all you want, but it's still going on out there in the real world, believe me. And you're wrong—I'm not casual about it at all. I'm damned serious."

She looked at him, her expression shuttered. "Is that what you think? That I live a sheltered little life unaware of what goes on in your 'real' world?"

His hand stilled its rotation of the yarn as something in her tone warned him he'd offended her. "I'm not indicting your life-style, Alex," he tried to reassure her. "I'm just trying to point out that there's a lot more ugliness out there than you think."

"Ah," she said noncommittally, still with that curious air of guardedness that hinted that something other than her seeming serenity was bubbling beneath the surface. But all she said was, "How did you get started as an agent, anyway?"

He stifled a yawn, his voice dropping to a low rumble as he relaxed, relieved to be back on neutral ground. "I spent my last year of college as an exchange student in West Berlin, where I became friends with another student, Joel Gibson. His father was the undersecretary at the American Embassy. After graduation, Joel's dad arranged for us to spend the summer earning some extra money as embassy couriers, and it just sort of grew from there. I think we both saw ourselves as junior James Bonds."

"But what about your college degree? Wasn't there something else you'd planned to do?"

His fingers stilled. Her question reminded him of the project he'd been working on up until last week, of the hours he'd poured into it during his medical leave. Equal parts anger and despair lanced through him at the reminder it was gone, lost forever with his stolen luggage, but the even cadence of his voice never changed. "I was an art major. Trust me, after graduation, there weren't any corporate recruiters clamoring to hire me. I didn't have to work, anyway. My dad had been well insured, and the money went into a trust his banker managed. When my mom died the winter of my junior year, she left me some investments, too. So," he concluded with an expressive shrug, "I could do pretty much whatever I wanted to."

"And you wanted to be a spy?" Alex's disbelief was evident in her voice.

He yawned, sliding lower in the bed. "I did then." The sheet bunched at his hip as he turned on his side to face her, settling his head into the pillow, his lazy gaze doing nothing for her heart rate.

"And now? What do you plan to do now that you're retiring?" To her dismay, his answer meant a lot to Alex. When had his future begun to matter to her? And why, for heaven's sake?

Instead of answering, his eyes fluttered shut, then he gave a telltale sigh and released his hold on the yarn, which dropped off the bed and rolled to Alex's feet.

She bent down to pick it up.

I do not care about this man, she told herself firmly. I'm simply doing him a favor, that's all. My concern is no different than it would be for any fellow human being.

So what if my heart turns over every time he gives me one of those rare smiles?

So what if a dozen times a day I find myself drifting toward his door so I can watch him while he sleeps?

So what if every night since he's been here I've laid awake imagining what it would be like to be in his arms?

It didn't mean she cared. It simply meant her girlfriends were right. She *had* been alone too long. She'd react this way to any man.

But staring down at the yarn clutched in her hands, yarn she'd purchased weeks ago in Phoenix, yarn she'd chosen from a vast variety of shades and hues, it was hard to convince herself of that particular truth.

Because the yarn wasn't just blue—it was an exact match of the glorious blue of Travis Cross's eyes.

Six

Travis recradled the phone, leaned back against the bunched bed pillows and forced his tense muscles to relax. So, LeClair had taken the bait. The crook was willing to believe that with the right persuasion—in this case, a half-million dollars—Travis might be convinced to betray the Department and sell him the diamonds.

A grim smile came and went on Travis's face. Although it was good to finally be doing something to aid LeClair's arrest, it was hardly a compliment to be so readily accepted as a man who'd sell himself to the highest bidder. Though why it should bother him now, when he'd played similar roles in the past without a pang, was a mystery.

He forced it from his mind, focusing on the next phase of the game. In forty-eight hours he would call LeClair again, at first pretending to have cold feet. Then, after he'd made the slimebag sweat a little, he'd commence to dicker, demanding even more money, then hinting right before he hung up that he'd found another buyer. Maybe he'd call back—and maybe he wouldn't. With any luck at all, Le-Clair, who was renowned for having a short fuse, would explode from the frustration.

A faint noise captured his attention. Instantly alert, he tried to define the sound. Unable to pinpoint it and not hearing it again, he began to relax, stretching his long legs and arching his spine as he tried to work out some of the kinks. "Blast it," he muttered, hitting his head on the headboard; lying in bed doing nothing was damned dangerous.

The noise came again, and this time he identified it as coming from the vicinity of the door. From years of practice, he held himself in check, muscles taut, his body coiled for action, his gaze locked on the door. Tensely, he waited.

There. There it was again.

The door opened an inch. Then another. And then another.

On a level with the doorknob, a shock of dark hair, the curve of a freckled cheek and one wide, bright brown eye materialized, and Travis relaxed. Brandon. Every day for the past week the kid had come over to "baby-sit" him while Sarah put Brandon's baby sister, Lizabeth, down for a nap.

"Hey, buddy," Travis said, scooting up in the bed and propping a pillow behind his back.

"You're awake," Brandon said, bounding into the room. He pulled a rumpled piece of paper from behind his back and held it out to Travis. "I brought you a picture."

Travis took the offering and Brandon immediately climbed up on the bed beside him. "This is great," Travis said, looking at the mass of blues and greens with blotches of beige here and there. He held it blue end up, hoping that was the sky.

"You know what it is? Huh? I painted me and my baseball team, the Sasquatch Sluggers. That's me right there." The boy pointed to the largest blob in the middle of the painting. He paused, then said apologetically, "I wanted to draw Sasquatch, but we had a mean old substitute today, and she said there was no such thing."

Travis, remembering similarly rigid, unimaginative teachers from his own childhood, spoke without thinking. "I could draw you one."

"Really?"

He shrugged, damning his wayward tongue. "Sure. You have a pencil?" he asked.

"You betcha." The youngster dug in his pocket and drew out a short, fat pencil stub.

Travis eyed it dubiously, then took it and grabbed the notepad lying next to the phone. "Why don't you tell me what you think Sasquatch looks like," he instructed Brandon, "and I'll try to draw it."

"Okay." Brandon's face screwed up with concentration. "Well, it's big, with little eyes and little ears and a huge nose—like a trumpet—and it's real hairy...." As the description grew more and more outlandish, the pencil flew faster and faster across the page until the legendary bigfoot took startling, if unconventional, shape.

"So what do you think?" Travis said finally, tipping the sheet a little to one side and studying it critically.

Brandon leaned against Travis's shoulder, staring wide-eyed at the outrageous character on the page. The hulking Sasquatch had small round eyes, a crooked smile and undeniable charm. "Wow!" the child said in awe. "How'd you do that?" He studied the picture a moment longer, then said, "It's rad, like—like Milton Monster. You should put your autogiraffe on it."

Autogiraffe? Travis cleared his throat. "I think you mean autograph, bud," he said, automatically scrawling his signature across the corner of the sketch. "There," he said, handing the pleased child the drawing. He sat back. "So, you play baseball, huh?" Travis had heard of Little League, but Brandon was hardly big enough to hold a bat.

"T-ball," Brandon explained. "Alex and my dad are the coaches, except Daddy can't be here very much. Right now he's in Minioctopus—"

Minioctopus? "Uh, Bran? Do you mean Minneapolis?"

"That's what I said. Anyway, he can't be at our game this weekend, and Auntie Alex tries but she's still learning, and besides, she's just a girl. Do you play baseball, Travis?"

"Yeah," Travis answered, thinking that calling Alex "just a girl" was a bit like calling the Empire State Building "just a shack."

"Good," the little boy said ingeniously. "Then you can help Auntie Alex."

Belatedly aware he'd just been drafted, Travis balked. "I don't think so," he told his young friend.

"Please, Travis?" the child wheedled.

Travis shot him a knowing look. "Brandon," he warned, then ruined it by adding, "I think we'd better talk to Alex."

"Okay," the little boy said with his charming smile, "but Auntie Alex'll say yes, I know she will."

Not if I get to her first. "We'll see."

When Alex opened the door, she found Brandon sitting cross-legged on the bed relating every last detail of his day to Travis, who, to his credit, was trying very hard to look attentive. In point of fact, he looked completely at home propped up in bed with the little boy beside him. For a man who liked to project a tough-guy image, he was acting very strange.

"Hi," she said, walking into the room. "I came to check on you two. How are you doing?"

"We're great!" Brandon answered for them both.

"Just great," Travis echoed, the edge of irony in his voice sailing right over Brandon's head.

"Look, Auntie Alex. Travis drew me a picture of Sasquatch," the child crowed, handing her the pencil drawing with a flourish.

Alex took the sheet of paper, glanced briefly at the sketch, then took a second, longer look, shocked by the extent of Travis's talent. With just a few strokes he'd created a magical creature, benevolent and inviting for all its bulk. "This is really good," she said sincerely, her gaze lifting curiously to Travis before coming back to the sketch. There was something about it, something almost familiar....

"Travis said, since Daddy's gonna be gone, he'd help you with T-ball if you'd let him, Auntie Alex."

Travis frowned, his eyes narrowing at Brandon's guileless expression. "Hold it, kid. That's not—"

"Yes, you did," Brandon interjected. "You said you would if Auntie Alex said it was okay. You'll let him help, won't you Auntie Alex?"

"Maybe Alex and I should discuss this," Travis ventured. "I've been sick, after all." He threw her a beseeching look over Brandon's head.

Still staring at the drawing, Alex said idly, "Oh, I don't think that will be a problem. I talked to the doctor this morning, and he assured me that by now you're probably no longer contagious. You're probably a little weak from being in bed, but once you're up and around, you'll get your strength back. The fresh air would do you a lot of good," she concluded, only then looking up. The glint in Travis's eyes told her instantly she'd said something wrong.

Brandon was no fool. Knowing enough to quit when he was ahead, he leapt off the bed. "Great! Then he can do it! I gotta go and tell Barry and Sean," he whooped, racing out of the room as if he were being chased by a pack of wolves.

Alex took one look at Travis's thunderous expression and was hot on the little boy's heels.

Why hadn't he just said no? Alex wondered the day of the game, stealing a quick glance at Travis's averted face as they roared down the county road in the Ferrari en route to the playing field. She'd been expecting him to do just that ever since she'd unwittingly trapped him into attending.

But he hadn't. For all his scowls and growls, there he sat, for which she was exceedingly glad.

She frowned, worrying that perhaps she was too glad. It was disturbing how much she'd come to like him in such a short time—and how much she dreaded his leaving. But leave he would; she had no illusions about that.

So why wasn't he gone? Despite some faint marks still blotching his skin, he was well on the road to full recovery. Actually, he seemed remarkably fit; his dark hair was shiny, even if it was so long it was curling over his collar and behind his ears, and if he was still feeling weak, you'd never guess it by the coiled energy emanating from him. She couldn't understand why he hadn't taken off already.

"You appear to be feeling better," she remarked, decided it was possible it hadn't occurred to him to tell her of his imminent departure. He probably wasn't accustomed to sharing his plans.

The gaze Travis turned to her was bland, but inside warning bells were going off. Was she getting ready to tell him to go?

He'd been preparing for just that possibility ever since she'd announced she'd spoken to the doctor, and he'd con-

sidered several different ways to forestall it. Deciding now
that a change of subject would serve best, he said, "Yeah,
I am," then added in the next breath, "I understand from
Brandon you were married. Childhood sweethearts?"

Alex blinked, uncertain she'd heard him right.

"Well?"

Obviously she had, but the question, coming as it did out
of left field, more than surprised her. It stunned her, enough
that she found her mouth answering before her brain had
time to think about it. "No. We met my sophomore year of
college at a lecture he was giving."

Travis's brow furrowed. "He was a professor?" What
had begun as a diversionary tactic was swiftly turning into
a topic of some interest.

Even as she wondered at his sudden personal interest,
Alex's face softened. "No. An inventor/entrepreneur. You
may remember him—he was a pioneer in personal computers, kind of like Billy Gates of Microsoft or Jobs and Woz-
niak of Apple. His name was Stefan Zbresky."

Travis recognized it instantly, something disturbing teasing at the back of his brain, but before he could zero in on
it, Alex continued. "We met at the university while I was an
undergraduate. He'd been invited to give a series of lec-
tures on the future of personal computers."

Although flattered when Stefan singled her out for
courtship, she'd been more than a little overwhelmed by his
success and the affluent life-style he enjoyed. She hadn't
been ready to make a commitment, much less get married
the way Stefan had wanted to soon after their third date. It
had been a year before she'd agreed to an engagement, and
another year until her graduation before they'd married.
Stefan had been impatient but grudgingly understanding;
Alex had been quick to point out they had their whole lives
to be married.

"Were you happy?" Travis asked now.

As happy as you could get for four whole days and seven hours. "Yes," Alex replied. Feeling the weight of his gaze, she kept her eyes glued firmly to the road.

"What happened?"

She shot him a glance, then brought her eyes back to the road. "He died." Usually that bald statement was more than enough to discourage even the most avid interest.

But not Travis. "How?" He knew it was rude, but didn't care. Hearing Zbresky's name had triggered something unpleasant in his memory—but he was damned if he could pin it down. Maybe, he thought, glancing at Alex, it was their marriage that had made the news and was teasing his memory; Zbresky had been a minor celebrity, and Alex was certainly beautiful enough to make the headlines.

"He was killed in an accident," she replied, no longer trying to mask her displeasure with his line of questioning.

That could be it, he decided. But before he had time to really think about it, she turned the tables by asking, "What about you?"

"Me what?" Travis said, as if it hadn't occurred to him that twenty questions could be played two ways.

His almost comic horror at being asked to explain himself went a long way toward alleviating Alex's pique. Her dimple flashed. "Have you ever been married?"

He shook his head decisively. "No way. I'm not a forever kind of guy." He braced his hands against the dash as they whipped around a corner. "Besides, the whole happily-ever-after thing is basically a bunch of hype, something advertising execs use to sell cars and toothpaste."

"I don't agree," Alex replied. "Men and women have been forming partnerships since the beginning of time. That basic, fundamental relationship is the cornerstone on which society gets its stability, and the belief in forever is what gives it the impetus to plan for the future, to hope. Every time a civilization discards that model, you get chaos, decay and, eventually, collapse. Look at ancient Rome.''

"I don't think I want to," Travis said, not bothering to disguise the amusement threading his low voice. "How about if I concede the basic argument—*Professor* Wright? With the addendum that, even given all that, it's not for somebody like me?"

"What do you mean, somebody like you?"

"Get real, lady. I'm hardly a good candidate for domestic bliss."

"But how do you know," she asked softly, pressing down on the accelerator as they shot down a particularly straight stretch of road, "if you don't try?"

He gave her a narrow look she couldn't quite define. "I may never have been married, but that doesn't mean I live like a monk. I even tried playing house once, even though, with my family history, I should've known better. It was a disaster. Beth was a really nice lady, and living with me brought her a world of hurt."

Beth? For some reason, hearing him pair himself with another woman, even if it was in the past, caused Alex more than a twinge of discomfort. Yet even as she dismissed the jealousy roiling through her as ridiculous, she felt compelled to contradict his conclusion. "But—"

He shook his head. "Give it up, lady. The bottom line is, I'm not the marrying type." As they rounded a curve, his body tipped toward hers. "In case you haven't noticed, I like having things my own way."

Alex found his closeness unnerving. She eased off the gas, slowing down because if he continued to stay so near it was just a matter of time before she began to hyperventilate. "I hadn't noticed," she lied, looking sideways at him.

Her breath froze in her chest as his dark blue eyes slid over her in a manner that was blatantly male. His gaze seemed to paint her with fire as it touched briefly on the thick rope of her hair, then burned downward, spreading heat over her throat, her breasts, her waist, finally coming to rest on her thighs, their shape faithfully outlined by her slim-fitting jeans. "Yeah, well, you'd better," he said softly.

Better what? Alex couldn't remember. She was going up in flames. In fascinated anticipation, she watched his hand move toward her. "Travis?" She wasn't certain if she'd managed to speak out loud or not.

She slowed the Ferrari even more. His hand was long fingered and beautifully male as it slid past her knee and settled high on her thigh. "God, Alex. You've got the most delicious legs."

His husky words sent a tremor rocketing through her. She turned the car off the road and wheeled to a stop, shifting into neutral and jerking on the safety brake. Her hands shook. She lifted her eyes to his face. "Travis...?" There was something she needed to tell him, but she couldn't quite remember what it was.

His hand caressed her, making languid little circles on the inseam of her jeans as his head began to descend towards hers. She knew he was going to kiss her, even when he said, "Damn it, you know this is all wrong...."

Was it? Perhaps, but as Alex's lashes fluttered shut and his lips touched hers, it didn't matter. This is what she'd been longing for, hungering for, for weeks.

Their arms locked around each other, Travis feverishly pulling her closer until her breasts were pressed against the hard wall of his chest. "Oh," she breathed, her mouth parting eagerly to welcome his tongue as his hand stroked over her braid and down her back.

He kissed her heatedly, with an almost desperate edge. Alex could feel the pounding of his heart, could hear the roughened cadence of his breathing. His open display of desire sent emotions sizzling through her like jolts of electricity: uncertainty, tenderness, passion—and a burgeoning sense of discovery.

He smelled wonderful, clean and male. But even as his lips worshiped hers, tasting, smoothing, demanding, something nagged at Alex. There was something different about this kiss; some subtle but fundamental change from the first one they'd shared that night in front of the hotel. That one had been exhilarating and exciting, teasing and tormenting. This kiss was all of that—but also something more.

She reached and laced her hands into the silk of his hair, thrilling to the need she could feel thrumming through him, answering her own. She tugged him closer, wishing away all the barriers between them, wanting him close, skin-to-skin, heartbeat to heartbeat. Heart to heart.

When did that happen? she wondered dazedly. When had this craving started, this longing to be joined body and soul to Travis Cross? When had she started to love him?

Before she could clarify the thoughts spiraling through her mind, his tongue nudged her teeth, slowly exploring before plunging deep, sending reality spinning away. She held tight to him as an anchor in the world gone mad, welcoming his possession, wanting his passion.

And then, without warning, the door was flung open, and Alex opened her eyes to a sea of little, bright-eyed-boy faces staring at her and Travis in openmouthed astonishment.

"Wow, gross!" Sean exclaimed, as Travis uttered a startled oath and flung himself back against the seat.

It was then that Alex remembered what it was she'd meant to tell Travis. "Hey, Travis?" she whispered, color high on her cheeks as she met his accusing stare. She tucked a loose wisp of pale blond hair behind her ear with fingers that shook. "We're here."

Seven

Alex was still feeling dazed an hour and a half later.

It was a perfect spring afternoon. The sun was shining, the aroma of freshly mown grass scented the air like Mother Nature's perfume, and for the first time ever, the Sasquatch Sluggers were actually winning a game.

I should be thrilled, Alex thought. But instead of exulting with her team, instead of cheering them on, she was still grappling with the incredible idea that had sprung up out of nowhere and now refused to go away.

She was in love with Travis Cross.

As she'd been doing repeatedly for the past ninety minutes, she trotted out all the arguments disputing the likelihood of such a conclusion, starting with his being all wrong for her—he'd spent years in the midst of violence, he didn't believe in love, he openly rejected the idea of marriage—and ending with his reaction if she ever confessed to such a feeling. Mr. Hands-off-don't-invade-my-space Cross would no doubt inform her unequivocally she was suffering the worst kind of delusion—and then probably clear out so fast he'd be at the end of the driveway before she got to the *e* in the word love.

None of which seemed to matter. Like it or not, want to or not, she loved him.

Which didn't change the fact that the wisest thing she could do was try to forget the whole thing.

And that would be a whole lot easier, she decided crossly, observing Travis through narrowed eyes as he stood a few feet away coaching Brandon whose turn it was at bat, if he would stop being so great with the kids and go back to behaving like a troll.

Instead, as Alex watched, Brandon—who up till now had never had a hit—connected the bat with the ball with an audible crack, and promptly turned to his mentor. "Hey, Travis! I did it!" Clutching the bat, the child began bouncing up and down as if his feet were on invisible springs. "I hit the ball!"

"You sure did," Travis said admiringly from his position on the baseline between home and first. "Now, lay down the bat, bud," he coached, "and run."

Brandon bolted. Little legs churning, he soon arrived at first.

"A single," Alex remarked like a calm, rational adult, moving closer to Travis like a moth drawn to a flame. "Pretty good."

"Yeah," he responded absently, rocking lightly up and down on his toes in a motion mildly reminiscent of Brandon's, his eyes riveted on the unfolding action. In the next instant the ball whizzed past the baseman's outstretched glove, and he went rigid, like a bird dog pointing his quarry. "Did you see that! *He missed the throw!*"

Alex stared at him in total amazement. He was less than a foot away. And he was bellowing.

Where, oh where, she wondered, feeling the pull of his charm at this unexpected but entirely endearing display of excitement, is my surly, monosyllabic stranger when I need him?

Entirely oblivious to her dilemma, Travis waved at Brandon and gestured frantically toward second. "Run!" he roared, his contained rocking motion deteriorating into something that closely resembled jumping up and down as the ball and Brandon simultaneously approached second.

Despite the fact that she was clearly in serious trouble, Alex couldn't seem to wipe the smile off her face. "Calm down," she teased. "This is grade-school T-ball, not the major leagues."

"A lot you know," he immediately contradicted, his body crackling with tension like an overloaded power line. "A game's a game. And *these* guys can't catch," he said with relish. "Look at that! *Now* they've missed the throw to second!" He cupped his hands at the sides of his mouth and screamed, "Go Brandon, go!"

But by now, Brandon had more than caught on. Hurtling toward third, when the ball once again sailed past the baseman's outstretched hands, the kindergartner knew exactly what to do. Tagging the base, he swept on toward home.

"*Yes!*" Travis yelled, triumphantly punching the air with his fist. "That's my boy!" Turning to Alex, he grasped her by the arms and whirled her around. At first in surprise, and then in awe, she stared at his jubilant expression, dizzy from a whole lot more than the mad way he was twirling her about.

She was still reeling when she stepped into her shower hours after the game. And as she pulled the glass door shut and moved beneath the spray, she could still see his face. His happy, incredibly appealing face.

All right, she thought, the water pounding against her back. Admit it. You're in serious trouble here. You've gone and fallen in love with an utterly gorgeous man. A man who makes your heart pound and your blood heat without any effort—and who'd rather have every tooth in his head ripped out than admit to even the possibility of the existence of lasting love.

So what, demanded the little voice in her head, *do you plan to do?*

Alex leaned her forehead against the cool tile, admitting with a heartfelt groan she didn't have the foggiest idea.

So relax, said the voice. *Go with the flow. Don't forget, it's been a long time since you've been with a man.*

Now *there* was some swell advice. Here she was, in love with a man to whom she was about as well suited as Little Orphan Annie was to Kevin Costner, and her conscience or subconscious or whatever it was, was saying inane things like *Go with the flow.*

Wondering what on earth was the matter with her, she picked up her bath sponge and began to scrub, starting at her toes and steadily working her way up.

But the voice didn't seem to have any intention of shutting up. *Alex,* it said gently, *there's nothing wrong with you. You're simply long overdue for a lover.*

She paused in her vigorous scrubbing and gave a little snort. Great! Another brilliant deduction. But then, what the heck, what was eight years without a man? Proof, perhaps, that she wasn't exactly a creature of unbridled passion?

But as she might have known, the voice had a snappy comeback for that, too. *Oh really?* it chided, still sounding irritatingly reasonable. *So what do you call what you and Travis were doing in the car? Oral aerobics?*

Oral aerobics? Oh, *please.* Alex scrubbed even harder.

The voice ignored her waspishness. *Quit being such a prude. Just look at your bedroom. Did you decorate it in a safe little floral print? No. Rudolph Valentino would feel right at home. It's the creation of a sleeping goddess of love, just waiting for the right man to come along and wake her up.*

Alex inhaled a gulp of water. Goddess of love? Good Lord—her psyche had gone off the edge.

Does Doris Day drive a Ferrari? Would Mother Theresa pick up a strange man in a parking lot?

"I did not pick Travis up!" she snapped, then caught herself before she said another word. Terrific. Now she was talking to herself. Out loud. This was definitely getting out of hand.

Oh, grow up, Alex. The voice finally sounded exasperated. *The question is, do you want to make love with Travis or not?*

The answer wiped every other thought right out of her head.

Did she want to make love with Travis?

Were there twenty-four hours in a day? Did summer follow spring? Did the sun rise in the east?

Of course she *wanted* to make love with him, she thought. For the first time in her life she'd met a man who could send her pulse rate off the charts with a single look.

So what kind of fool passes up that kind of passion? asked the voice.

Her kind, perhaps?

As was her habit, she started weighing pros and cons, trying to list the advantages of an affair against going on alone, but again the voice intervened.

*Give it up, Alex. It's time to let go. To live a little. You're
alive and Stefan's dead—and what happened to him wasn't
your fault.*

She knew that.

*Maybe so. But then why are you still punishing yourself?
When are you going to quit pretending your life is complete
when in reality all you're doing is living vicariously through
other people?*

Oh! Of all the—! Alex's indignant reply was lost in a
startled yelp as the water suddenly turned icy cold while a
great grumbling moan issued from the pipes. "What the
heck!" she swore, fumbling at the taps as she frantically
tried to shut off the chilly water. The instant it was off, she
shoved open the glass door and leapt outside, her dripping
hair splattering droplets of water in a wide arc as she
snatched up a pale pink towel and clutched it to her shiver-
ing body.

From the other side of the common wall between the
master and the guest bath came the unmistakable groan of
water rushing into the tub.

She couldn't believe it. Quite clearly, Travis Cross, that
treacherous man, was running a bath. Hadn't they agreed
she'd shower first, he'd shower second?

Yes. But was he waiting? Not if the sounds from the next
room were any indication. The crazy man would probably
slip in the tub and knock himself silly, and then where would
they be? She'd have to call the girls to help lift him out. God
help them both, then.

On some level she knew she was being ridiculous. Travis
had just spent an afternoon fending off a horde of little
boys. Compared to that, he could probably shoot Snoqual-
mie Falls in the bathtub and walk away unscathed.

But for some reason, her ability to think logically seemed
to have gone out the window with the shower steam.

Wrapping a dry towel around her hair, she shrugged into a short, rose-colored terry robe and headed for the other bathroom with the determination of a commanding general, careless of the watery trail she left behind. Barely registering the open door, she righteously stormed in. And ran smack into Travis's naked back.

With a startled squeak, she jumped back.

Travis turned, looming over her. "Alex?" His voice trailed away as he looked from her water-beaded face to the delicately flushed skin of her throat, then dropped lower still to the long expanse of her legs, shown to advantage by the short robe.

Alex's heart rate soared, her anger evaporating as she became conscious of the brevity of her attire. "I thought you were in the bathtub," she said lamely, clutching her lapels.

Travis's brows rose speculatively. "Yeah? Were you coming to join me?"

She stared at him, fighting the impulse to let her gaze drift below his chin. "No."

"Oh. You came to watch?"

"No! I . . ." In a move dictated more by self-preservation than actual curiosity, she shifted to the left, peering around his shoulder and taking in the bubbles billowing from the tub, surrounding a clutch of floating baseball bats. Her eyes widened as she noted the open bottle of her favorite bubble bath perched precariously on the ledge of the tub enclosure.

Her gaze jerked back to Travis. "You're crazy. The pox has gone to your brain. Do you realize you're bathing baseball bats in ten-dollar-an-ounce designer bubble bath?"

Travis shifted, moving closer. "Oh, I'm crazy all right." His breath tickled across her cheek. "But it's got nothing to do with baseball or bubble bath."

Alex took her first real look at him since entering the room. Her soaring heartbeat froze.

Draped in nothing but damp black nylon gym shorts, he was only a designer label shy of naked. She stepped back, bumping up against the vanity.

Something in his expression altered, his eyes darkening to a sultry shade of midnight. "Alex." With deliberate intent, he took a step nearer, reaching with an arm rippling with muscle to tug the towel from her hair.

"I...I would have washed the bats," she said inanely.

"*Alex.*" He pressed up against her, his hands gently cupping her shoulders as he looked intently into her eyes. "I'm going to leave soon. Do you understand? I'm not a forever kind of guy."

What she knew was that he was going to kiss her and, just as it had both other times he'd touched her, passion erupted inside her like champagne blowing a cork. She couldn't breathe, she couldn't think—and she didn't care. Only one thing mattered. To get closer to Travis, to his heat, his warmth, his touch. "I know you are," she whispered. "I...it doesn't matter." And in that moment, she knew she meant it.

Perhaps it was because of what had happened to Stefan, but Alex suddenly knew she wasn't willing to forfeit certain happiness now against the mere chance of an unlikely future. She'd made that mistake once before, postponing the opportunities of today against the possibilities of tomorrow, only to learn to her sorrow tomorrow could disappear with the speed of a ricocheting bullet.

She didn't intend to make the same mistake twice, and her conviction was clear in the glowing, amber gaze she turned up to Travis. Recognizing it, he pulled her firmly into his heated embrace and laid claim to her mouth, his hands threading through the damp, silky strands of her hair. With a slight tug, he tipped her head back, deepening the angle of the kiss. When her mouth opened on a rush of pleasure, his tongue dipped inside.

Alex pressed feverishly against him. She let go of her robe, her modesty as forgotten as her doubts. She flattened her palms against the smooth, firm flesh of his chest. With an audible sigh of pleasure, she explored the pectorals she'd previously only admired. He was all warm, masculine power, beautifully defined.

Was it wrong, she wondered fleetingly, to desire him so much when he'd made it clear he wanted no more than a temporary alliance?

No, she thought, her panic receding as swiftly as it'd arrived, replaced by the certainty that within the warm circle of Travis's embrace, she had nothing to lose and everything to gain.

Trailing her hands down his sleek sides, she surrendered to temptation and locked her arms around his waist.

Travis groaned, breaking the kiss. "Oh, lady," he whispered, his lips gliding up the smooth skin of her throat to nuzzle behind her ear, while his hands traced down the delicate line of her spine. At the dip of her back, his fingers splayed out, molding the terry of her robe to the curve of her behind.

"Travis," Alex said urgently.

"I know," he said, his teeth nipping the bottom lobe of her ear while his hands delved beneath the hem of her robe. "Oh, lady, do I know," he said on an exhalation of breath, running the pads of his fingertips up the backs of her thighs.

Alex's knees buckled. Instinctively her hands rose and curled around his neck.

Travis's hands closed on her derriere. With a controlled surge of power, he lifted her to the vanity and stepped into the cradle of her thighs.

As if by their own volition, Alex's fingers feathered over the back of his neck, then skimmed down the taut flesh of his arms. Clasping his left hand, she raised it to her mouth and pressed a languid, openmouthed kiss to the pulse throbbing wildly on the inside of his wrist.

Travis gave a violent shudder. "Stop that," he ordered. He took a half-step back, his eyes nearly black with desire as he took in Alex's flushed cheeks and tumbled hair. Holding her gaze with his own, his hands moved to the front of her robe and carefully inched it open. Deliberately teasing them both, he continued to stare deep into her eyes as he peeled the damp cotton away from her glowing skin.

When the robe draped loosely off her shoulders, he still refused to look down. Instead, he grasped thick handfuls of her gleaming hair and smoothed it, with painstaking care, over the quivering lure of her full, naked breasts.

Alex gave a strangled little moan. Her back arched, her lashes fluttered closed.

Travis dropped his gaze, his hands tightening in her hair as he drank in his first sight of the pink-and-gold treasure he'd uncovered. When Alex grasped his shoulders, offering herself in abandoned trust, his head dipped as if weighted, unerringly finding her tightly beaded nipple and bestowing upon it a reverent, heated kiss before his lips parted and he hungrily began to suckle. Beneath his questing lips, her skin was taut and sweet and fragrant.

Alex bowed in his arms, nearly coming up off the counter at the exquisite but foreign sensation. "Oh," she gasped, anchoring him to her by the hands she thrust into his hair, forgetting to breathe as tendrils of sensation swept from the tip of her breast to the jointure of her thighs, twisting tighter and tighter with each demanding pull of his mouth. Her head fell back, thrusting her pelvis forward, her hair pouring like molten gold over his arm as her legs wrapped around the hard columns of his thighs. With an instinct as old as time, she pressed against him, meeting the unyielding proof of his need with a languid roll of her hips that quickly had them both shuddering for breath.

Travis released his hold on her breast and rocked back on his heels, towering above her, surveying the turgid nipple still damp from the attention of his lips.

"Travis?" she said, not certain what to make of his fierce expression.

"Not yet," he said hoarsely. With hands that shook, he reached out and cupped both her breasts, then leaned over and slowly ran the tip of his tongue along the deep valley he'd created between his hands. As his mouth reached the V where her collarbones met, his hands settled low on her back. He pressed her closer, burying his face against the soft skin behind her ear. "I want you, Alex."

Her hands moved restlessly across the broad contour of his back, her slender fingers sketching the sleek muscles divided by his spine. "Yes," she said simply. But she knew if he made her wait much longer, she'd soon be reduced to begging.

Travis squeezed his eyes shut, saying a fervent prayer of thanks for her answer—and for his trip to the men's room at the playing field where he'd caught Sean showing the other boys what great water balloons his older bother's condoms made. For the first time in his law-enforcement career, it looked like he'd actually confiscated something he could use.

Straightening, he took a half pace back, his eyes seeking Alex's as he hooked his thumbs in the elasticized waistband of his shorts and pushed them down over his hips, kicking them away as they hit the floor. A glint of amusement danced in his eyes as Alex's pupils widened at her first sight of his masculinity, the glint deepening to a gleam as a blush heated her cheeks when he made swift use of Sean's bounty.

He reached out and helped her strip off her robe, then took a step closer and gathered her back into his arms.

His lips sought hers, soft and fragrant and yielding, his hands sliding again beneath her derriere, supporting her as she pressed eagerly forward to meet him. And then he was home, filling her with himself, and finding himself filled in the taking.

It was almost too good. For a minute, the reality of being gloved in her body was so exquisite Travis feared he was going to go off like a teenager. But then he looked down into Alex's upturned face, and the wonder and rapture evidenced by her closed eyes, flushed cheeks and sweetly parted lips steadied him.

He began to move. Slowly at first, giving her time to adjust to him, and then faster, more powerfully, meeting the answering push of her hips with unrestrained hunger.

His rhythm intensified when he caught their reflection in the mirror. Against the delicate line of her back, his hands were big, dark and long fingered, and with every powerful thrust of his body into hers, her hair swept across his forearm like liquid silk. His body dwarfed hers, framing her slim, elegant curves; he was bronze to her ivory, ebony to her gold, hard where she was soft and solid where she was sleek, and the image of their joining was suddenly more than he could take. His lips sought hers, his mind refusing to analyze why he was suddenly so desperate to be connected to her in every way he could.

Alex came apart in his arms.

Like a sunrise, it started for her with a tiny pinprick of light, a faint glimmer of energy promising untold delight. Then everything inside her seemed to lighten, to focus on that slowly growing energy as it gathered strength, building until it burst into incredible, radiant life. She was bathed in its warmth, illuminated by its brilliance, redefined by its glow, and as she flung her head back, her amber eyes opened, mirroring her passion and totally destroying what was left of Travis's control. With a last powerful thrust, he breached the final barrier between them and joined her in the light.

Long minutes later they were still tangled together, arms and legs entwined, breaths mingled, hearts beating in synchronization.

From somewhere far away came the faint sound of a door swinging closed.

Travis barely heard it. His thick, black lashes fanned his cheeks as he rested his forehead against Alex's, savoring a sense of completion he'd never before experienced. For the first time in his life, he understood why men sometimes made promises of everlasting love after sex. If they experienced anything even remotely resembling what he and Alex had just shared, he couldn't blame them for trying to attain a lifetime of such ecstasy.

Except that it never seemed to work out that way.

Of course, that didn't mean he was adverse to making love to Alex again. Soon, he decided, in the instant before his attention was claimed by a faint pattering sound.

What the hell was that? Reluctantly, he lifted his head from Alex's flushed skin and cocked an ear toward the door. The pattern turned into a steady thump, which seemed to be getting louder.

A little V formed between his brows as he concentrated, trying to decide what it was he was hearing. Stairs. Someone was coming up the stairs.

Someone was coming up the stairs?

Gently but swiftly, he extricated himself from Alex. Then he exploded into action, leaping at the door in a single, incredible bound, slamming it shut with all the weight of his body behind it while Alex stared at him in astonishment.

Before she could utter a word, much less demand an explanation, a tentative knock sounded at the door. "Travis?" came a familiar little voice. "Are you in there?" *Brandon.* Alex turned a delicate pink from the tips of her toes to the top of her head and dove for her robe.

Travis took a deep, calming breath. Even so, when he did manage to speak, he still sounded like a man who'd just run a cross-country marathon. And lost. "What do you want?" he croaked.

"Can you come out and play?"

Alex slipped into the robe, glancing up just as Travis sent a harassed look her way before he rasped a no in a tone that discouraged debate.

Unfortunately Brandon didn't appear to get the message. There was only the barest pause before he asked, "Why not?"

Travis's eyes scrunched into slits as he searched for patience. "Because," he said finally. "I'm busy."

"Yeah?"

"Yeah."

"Oh. What are you doing? Can I help?"

"No." The single word was fierce and uncompromising.

Brandon wasn't fazed in the least. "Oh," he said innocently. "Are you going to be done soon?"

"Yes," Travis gritted out. "Damn it," he added under his breath.

At his mournful tone, the absurdity of the situation began to assert itself on Alex. A reluctant smile tugged at the corners of her mouth as Brandon went on persistently,

"Then are you coming over for the victory party? My mom says it's gonna be the best acceleration you've ever seen."

Travis sighed. "Brandon?"

"Yes?"

"I think you mean celebration, buddy."

"Yep, that's what I said. An acceleration with cake and ice cream and everything."

Travis rested his forehead on the door. "Go home, kid."

"You promise you'll be over soon?"

"I promise."

"Okay." There was a pregnant pause and then the child said, "Uh, Travis?"

"What?"

"Can you bring Auntie Alex? I can't find her anywhere."

"I'll bring her."

"Okay. See ya later, alligator."

Travis listened, waiting for the sound of footsteps, but nothing happened.

"See ya later, alligator." There was no mistaking the anticipatory note in Brandon's voice.

Just as there was no mistaking Travis's mystification. Clearly, he knew something was expected of him, but it was also obvious he didn't have the vaguest idea what.

From across the room Alex supplied in a choked whisper, "In a while, crocodile."

Their gazes met, hers glittering with repressed mirth, his with a combination of exasperation, impatience and disbelief. He leaned his head back against the door, rolling his eyes at the ceiling. "In a while, crocodile," he intoned between his teeth.

Mercifully Brandon left—and not a second too soon.

At the sound of his retreating footsteps, Alex finally lost the tight hold she'd been keeping on herself and slid bonelessly down the vanity front, clutching the edges of her robe together as she dissolved in a fit of smothered laughter.

Travis stared at her in wonder.

Eight

Dressed in a pair of snug black jeans and a black knit shirt, Travis's eyes watered from the smoke issuing from the barbecue on Sarah's back porch. Standing as he was before the grill, he was completely hemmed in by a chattering pack of small boys, while Brandon's two-year-old sister clung like a limpet to his hip, her skinny little arms wrapped in a death grip around his neck.

Where was Brandon, anyway? he wondered a little desperately. And what was *he* doing, slinging burgers for a bunch of suburban strangers? Gently removing Lizabeth's finger from his ear, he thought gloomily, *All I need is a cardigan, and my impersonation of Mr. Rogers will be complete.*

He frowned as he spied Alex across the lawn, talking to a trio of women—a tall brunette, a flashy, older blonde and the woman who'd driven him from the hospital, Connie, he thought her name was, who was wearing an incredibly ugly red dress. His frown deepened as he thought about the steady stream of questions he'd been asked by Alex's neighbors about their relationship. The way they acted, you'd have thought they were Alex's family and had every right to demand to know his intentions. He could imagine the collective reaction if it were known he'd made love to her—in the bathroom. They'd barbecue him; hell, they'd *fricassee* him.

But how could he have known that Alex, nice, all-American, apple-pie-wholesome Alex, would melt from his kiss like a candle hit by a blowtorch? Who would have guessed that beneath her cool Grace Kelly looks and her Donna Reed philosophy of life, a *Madonna* like sexuality smoldered, just waiting to burst into flame?

The woman was clear, unadulterated, hundred-proof trouble. Hadn't he known it right from the start? From that very first encounter, hadn't she been able to get under his skin, to turn his usual chilly rationality into something about as cool and predictable as an erupting volcano? And every time he got her pegged, got her placed in a nice, safe little category where he felt he could deal with her, didn't she reveal some new aspect of herself that left him scrambling to keep up? She had more twists and turns than a contestant in a dance contest.

Sean tugged on his shirt. "I still don't get it," he said in that petulant tone that grated on Travis's nerves like a fingernail across a blackboard. "If birds and airplanes can fly, why can't I?"

Travis gave a sigh, more than a little exasperated at being asked to answer a question he'd already answered three times. "Because. It's a principle of aerodynamics. Mass versus—"

"Hi, guys." Alex waved a hand in a fruitless attempt to dissipate the smoke and smiled at the grateful look Travis sent her way. "Can I borrow Mr. Cross for a few minutes? There's someone who wants to meet him." She reached up and peeled Lizabeth's arms from his neck, transferring the child to Sarah who was walking by on her way to the kitchen.

"Thanks," Sarah said, sticking out her tongue as she bustled away.

"Thanks," Travis echoed far more sincerely.

"Don't thank me yet," Alex murmured in an undertone as she led him over to the brunette he'd seen her talking to earlier. "Travis, this is Dawn," she said. Although her tone was polite, her eyes twinkled at him wickedly.

He wondered what was going on as he took the hand the woman offered him and said politely, "Nice to meet you, Dawn."

Dawn was tall and broad shouldered, and he got part of his answer when she grabbed his fingers with a grip like a vise and refused to let go. "I'm thrilled to make your acquaintance," she trilled, in a coy little voice suited to a woman half her size. "My son speaks so highly of you, unlike some other people—" she gave Alex a brief malevolent look "—whose names I won't mention."

Travis gave a silent whistle, wondering what Alex had done to warrant such enmity while trying to guess which of the boys was the brunette's.

He didn't have long to speculate as the woman tightened her grip on his hand and said coquettishly, "I'm Sean's mother. You know—Sean Lawn."

Dawn and Sean *Lawn?* It was the first time he'd heard the little bully's last name—and no wonder. He crooked an eyebrow at Alex, who, if she was bothered by Mrs. Lawn's hostility, wasn't letting it show. Instead, her eyes were fairly dancing at him as she said blandly, "I believe you've already met Dawn's husband...John?"

John Lawn? Travis had to clear his throat before he could speak. "Ah, yes, I did. Earlier. I believe he was with your daughter," he said, addressing Mrs. Lawn.

"Oh, yes. He and Fawn are devoted to each other. Fathers and daughters, you know? Now me, I tend to get along best with our boys. But then Ronnie and Sean are my treasures, even if some people—" she threw another venomous look Alex's way "—don't think so. Of course," she addressed Travis, although her words were obviously for Alex, "so often people who have no children of their own don't understand a mother's devotion or a child's natural playfulness. Don't you agree, Travis?"

His eyes narrowed dangerously as he decided he'd about had it with this woman's not-so-subtle jabs at Alex, a wolfish grin flitting across his face as he anticipated her reaction when he told her about the "balloons" her "treasure" had been playing with earlier today. "Oh, I don't know," he said, refusing to consider why he felt this foreign compulsion to protect Alex, who, as if sensing what he intended to do, was applying a steady pressure to his forearm in a silent attempt to stop him. Ignoring her, he said silkily, "I suppose it depends on your definition of playful. Personally, I don't think a six-year-old has any business using—"

"Look!" Alex interrupted urgently, nearly yanking his arm out of the socket as she tried to jerk him away. She continued loudly, "Excuse us, Dawn, but Sarah is waving at us. She must need something. *Now*." The last word hinted at such dire consequences if Travis didn't comply he had to smile as he let her drag him away.

He grinned down at her, his eyes gleaming knowingly as they crossed the yard. "Coward," he said so low she was the only one who could hear him.

"Shh," Alex said dauntingly.

"Oh, all right," he conceded, his eyes playing lazily over her flushed cheeks, lingering momentarily on her lips, still slightly swollen from his earlier kisses. She had her hair piled loosely on top of her head in a relaxed Gibson Girl sort of upsweep, and she was wearing a body-hugging T-shirt dress that did alarming things to his blood pressure. His finger followed the path of a tendril that had escaped, tracing it down the silky column of her slim throat. He cleared his suddenly tight throat. "So."

Alex stared at him; the color in her cheeks increased as she read the burgeoning desire in his blue, blue eyes.

"What did you do to earn Dawn Lawn's undying admiration?" he inquired, while his eyes asked something entirely different.

Her lips parted in involuntary answer to his unspoken question, her body straining toward his. "I—"

Two members of the Sasquatch Sluggers raced by, reminding Alex where she was. She stepped back, moved blindly to the picnic table a few feet away and hastily began gathering up the used paper plates and cups, struggling for composure.

Good Lord! She'd nearly thrown herself into Travis's arms, all but begging him with her eyes to kiss her! She struggled to remember what he'd asked. "I made the mistake of telling her the truth about her 'treasure,'" she said, when it finally came back to her. "I can't abide lying under any circumstances, and Sean has never learned to tell the truth." Arms loaded with litter, she looked around for somewhere to discard it. "He told me one fib too many, and I suspended him for two games. Dawn has never forgiven me."

"Ah. One of those." Travis took the plates and cups from her hands and tossed them into a strategically placed trash can, telling himself the sudden knot in his stomach was from the pair of hamburgers he'd consumed. His back to Alex, he said with forced nonchalance, "So you've got a thing about liars, huh?"

Alex whisked crumbs off the table with her hand. "I guess you could put it that way," she said, placing a jar of mustard on top of the paper napkins to anchor them against the light breeze that had blown up. "Lying seems so pointless, somehow. If people were honest with each other up front, a lot of pain could be avoided later on."

"Yeah, but everybody lies," he observed. "Didn't I overhear you assuring Connie, when she asked, that you liked her dress? And don't you really think she looks like a giant, talking tomato?"

"Travis!" she hissed.

But when he raised a brow in silent challenge, she had to concede, sending him a look of amused resignation.

"Okay, I admit that even I occasionally tell white lies, the kind meant to spare someone else's feelings. But what I'm talking about, what I can't tolerate, are self-serving lies, the kind that only benefit the liar." Seeing his suddenly guarded look, she tried to clarify further. "That kind of lying makes me crazy, and the kids all know that it's the one thing I won't put up with. I always tell them I don't care what it is they've done—I can always find a way to forgive an honest mistake—just don't lie to me."

"Yeah, but..." Before he could pursue the matter further, Brandon came bounding up, launching himself at Travis's chest with a whoop.

"I thought you'd never get here!" the child exclaimed, wrapping his arms around Travis's neck for a hug, then leaning over and planting a big kiss on Alex's cheek. He gave her a stern look. "Where were you? I looked everywhere."

Alex and Travis exchanged a look before Alex said simply, "I was busy."

Brandon's expression grew speculative. "That's what grown-ups always say when they don't want to give you an answer," he remarked with a wisdom beyond his years.

"And you'll say the same things when you grow up," Travis said, effectively changing the subject by giving the boy a slight toss in the air that caused him to give a delighted squeal. Catching him, Travis turned Brandon around, then held him upside down, bringing on a series of high-pitched giggles, before finally setting him on his feet.

The little boy latched onto Travis's hand. "Will you come see my room? Please? It's rad—I've got bunk beds and everything." He turned to Alex. "You, too, Auntie Alex. Mommy got my poster framed," he enthused, dragging the two adults into the house and up to his small, cheery bedroom decorated in bright primary colors. "See!" he exclaimed, the instant they'd cleared the threshold. "Isn't it neat?"

Alex, who'd logged a lot of time in Brandon's room, merely nodded, focusing her attention on the newly framed poster of Milton Monster across the room as the two males discussed the advantages of bunk beds. Although Milton was a charming creature with his gentle eyes and crooked smile, it was the picture of Sasquatch Travis had drawn— which was taped to the wall next to the poster—that drew her across the room. As she studied the pencil drawing, she was only vaguely aware of Brandon's demand that Travis try out the upper bunk.

There was something so *familiar* about the style of the drawing, she decided, her gaze drifting back toward the Milton poster. It was almost as if…as if, she thought slowly, recognition dawning, it had been drawn by the same person who'd drawn Milton. Even as she cocked her head, noting the similarities between the two mystical creatures, her mouth curved at the idea of her big, bad secret agent writing a children's book.

Still . . . she couldn't seem to help it when her eyes sought the distinctive signature Travis had scrawled across the bottom of his Sasquatch drawing. There were the first few letters of his first name and then simply an X—a cross—for his last name. Knowing she was being ridiculous, she turned to the poster, but she found no answers there; the bottom of it had been cropped to fit the frame and the artist's signature was gone.

It was ludicrous, anyway. She knew the name of the author of *The Great Beyond*, and it wasn't Travis Cross. It was Triggs or Trips or Tracks—something like that—

"Come on, Auntie Alex!" Brandon yelled, demanding her attention. He patted the top-bunk mattress, indicating she should join him.

"I don't think so," Alex said, her eyes going from the little boy to the large man lying propped on one elbow behind him.

"What's the matter, Auntie Alex?" Travis asked with an edge of challenge. "Afraid of heights?"

Alex looked pointedly at his tall frame filling most of the available space on the mattress, the wicked gleam in his dark blue eyes as he met her gaze bringing a faint flush to her cheeks. "Nope. Just not enough space."

"There's plenty of room," Brandon countered, placing his hands on Travis's chest and pushing, as if he could stuff his big friend into the crack between the side of the bed and the wall. "See?"

"Yeah. See?" Travis mimicked in mock seriousness.

Knowing it was probably a mistake but not being one to back down from a challenge, Alex hiked up the skirt of her dress and scaled the small ladder, then shook her head skeptically as she saw the narrow space left to her.

"What's the matter?" Travis asked, a brow rising in polite inquiry. "The extra brownie you ate after that monster cheeseburger go straight to your hips?"

"All right, that's it," she retorted, scrambling onto the bed, only to find herself teetering on the edge, wondering where to go next.

"Here," Brandon said, scooting closer to Travis and patting the four-inch wide swatch of mattress available to her. With a sigh, she maneuvered herself into the narrow space, facing Travis with Brandon wedged between them.

The little boy grinned happily. "This is nice. I have to sleep on the bottom 'cuz Mommy's afraid I might fall out. But I like the top. What do you like, Travis? Do you like to be on the bottom or the top?"

"Oh, I don't know," he replied, his eyes darkening as his gaze probed Alex's. "I'm . . . flexible." His gaze turned smoky, and Alex felt the look he turned on her all the way to her toes.

"What about you, Auntie Alex?" Brandon asked innocently. "What do you think?"

"I think I'm getting down," she said calmly, only the huskiness of her voice betraying her agitation as she twisted around and jumped gracefully to the ground.

Her heart was racing, and it wasn't from the leap off the bed. When Travis looked at her that way, it was as if her body developed a will of its own; in just the brief space of the last few seconds, her nipples had peaked against the soft fabric of her dress, while a tingling warmth had started to gather at the apex of her thighs, even though this was hardly the time or the place for either reaction.

"Wow!" Brandon exclaimed admiringly. "You jumped. That's cool. I want to jump. Can I jump, too?"

Reluctantly turning around, Alex said, "Sure, but just this once. And you'd better let me catch you." The words had barely left her mouth before Brandon flung himself off the bed and into her hastily outstretched arms.

She was still trying to catch her breath when Travis said quietly from above her, "What about me? Will you catch me, too?" and before she could reply, before she could do more than glance up at him, he was leaping lightly down.

He landed practically on top of her, his arms closing around her for balance, his big, hard body pressed intimately to her softer one. "Oops," he said gently. Alex's eyes flew to his, but it didn't take the heat she saw there to tell her he was as affected by her as she was by him. Standing as close as they were, she had other more substantial proof.

As if of their own volition, her fingers stroked the smooth, warm skin stretched taut across his biceps, and she marveled at how much this man had come to mean to her in such a short space of time. "Let's go home," she said quietly, the enormity of her feelings overpowering her.

At her words, his entire body tightened. "Are you sure?" he probed, unwittingly asking the same question he'd put to her in the bathroom only hours earlier.

Then as before, any uncertainties Alex harbored evaporated under the heat of his gaze. "Yes," she said.

It was as simple as that. Ushering Brandon downstairs and out into the yard, Alex signaled to Sarah that they were leaving, and they slipped discreetly away to Alex's house, which they entered through the back door. During the time they'd been in Brandon's room dusk had fallen, and the house was dark except for the light above the stove. Hands clasped, they moved through the shadows to the stairs that led to the bedrooms.

Alex's bedroom had figured prominently in Travis's fantasies from the first moment he'd seen it, but now, as he stood in the doorway, watching Alex light the trio of candles on her bureau, reality began to swiftly outclass his imagination.

The candlelight painted the walls, dancing and shifting from the soft breeze wafting in through the bank of open windows. The leaves of the numerous palm and ficus trees around the room rustled, waving gently and casting dappled shadows on the walls. In a tree outside, a night bird sang.

Travis found he couldn't move as Alex stripped off her dress, dropping it to the floor in silent invitation before pulling the pins from her hair, as beautiful as a living statue as she stood silhouetted against the black velvet night beyond the windows. Looking up, finding him watching her, she gently shook her head, sending her hair tumbling in a shimmer of gold to her waist. "Well, hell," he said hoarsely. In three quick strides he was across the room, burying his hands in that golden splendor, drinking in the fragrance of her skin, which was more exciting than any aphrodisiac.

She pushed him slightly away. "Don't you think you're a little overdressed?" she asked, unable to believe her own boldness. She was out of control, but until he'd taken her in his arms earlier that day, she hadn't realize how starved she was for a man's touch. How, she wondered now, had she gone so long without this pleasure, this intimacy, this fire sweeping through her blood?

She knew the answer. It wasn't any man she craved; it was only Travis Cross. She loved him.

She undid the buttons at the neck of his pullover shirt.

"Oh, yes," he rasped, a little surprised by his own eagerness.

Alex understood; her own body seemed to have forgotten it had been totally satiated only hours earlier as she tugged the tail of the shirt free of his jeans and yanked the

black cotton knit impatiently up his torso, pausing briefly
to admire the enticing section of bronzed midriff she'd uncovered. Yet even that slight delay was too much. In record
time, she divested him of his shoes, shirt and jeans, until he
stood before her wearing nothing more than narrow navy
briefs.

"You're so beautiful," she breathed, watching in fascination as a thin flush of color washed across his cheekbones at her words.

He cupped her chin in his palm, tracing down her cheek
with his thumb. "This was all I could think of at that damn
barbecue," he confessed.

The raw hunger in his voice as much as the words took the
starch right out of Alex's knees. "Me, too," she whispered.

His hand drifted urgently from the shell-pink lace of her
bra to the matching silk of her French-cut bikini panties
before he swept her into his arms. "Hell," he said, the
words muffled as he hungrily sought her mouth, "I'm going to be lucky to make it to the bed as it is."

"I hope so." Alex's lips parted as she eagerly welcomed
his kiss, feeling inflamed by his taste, intoxicated by the
clean, male scent of his skin. She couldn't seem to get
enough of him, the low rumble of his voice, the heat radi-
ating off his taut skin and the feel of all that resilient muscle underneath her fingertips combining to condense her
world to nothing but him.

As he laid her down in the center of the lush velvet bedspread, stripping away their remaining clothes in the space
of a heartbeat, she realized what she felt for him was a mature woman's abiding passion, and she knew, in the inherent way of women, that while what she'd felt for Stefan had
been sincere, it was still only a pale version of the vivid
emotions Travis painted on her heart.

The knowledge fueled her need for him. There would be time enough later for more leisurely love play, for soft words and slow touches, for learning and teaching and explanations. But for now, swept away by an urgency she couldn't control, by the fire raging through her blood and the cry for completion in her soul, Alex could only gasp as he came down on top of her, big and dark and lithe. With instinct as her guide, she twisted beneath Travis, enticing him, imploring him, inciting him. She wanted him. Now.

Her hands stroked over the slick muscle of his back; she rocked him in the cradle of her thighs. "Travis," she said fiercely.

"I'm sorry," he rasped, his breath coming like a bellows, "I just can't wait. Next time, lady..."

Her arms tightened around him. "Don't. Don't wait. Not now," she implored. "I need you."

"Alex." Her name was an entreaty, a prayer, an exclamation of wonder all in one as his body claimed hers in one long, smooth thrust.

She arched off the bed, crying out at their joining, and in the space of that instance she became a part of him, an extension of the strong arms holding her protectively, at one with the powerful rhythm driving his body. Pleasure spiraled through her like a rising tide, growing with every forward thrust, intensifying with each agonizing retreat until it claimed her like a flood. Deluged by a wash of sensation, she was swiftly overcome by the tidal wave of pleasure. "Travis," she cried, and the absolute wonder in her voice, no less than the resplendence of her body, triggered Travis's own release. With a harsh exclamation of pleasure, he shuddered to a climax.

Moments later, he collapsed with a gusty sigh, twisting onto his back to lie beside her. As if it was the most natural thing in the world, she rolled toward him, taking shelter in the curve of his arm. She felt him tense, but before she could ask what was wrong, he relaxed, pulling her closer, his hand splaying possessively across her hip. "Mmm," she murmured, her voice lazy with satisfaction as she pressed a soft butterfly kiss to the side of his neck. "That was wonderful."

And to Travis's utter stupefaction, she gave him a meltingly sweet smile and fell promptly to sleep.

He made a mental note to tell her in the morning that it was the guy who was supposed to cork out.

Nine

Illuminated by a shaft of moonlight, Alex slept stretched on her side, her beautiful face cradled on one slim arm, her sleep as serene and peaceful as an innocent child's.

Standing in the shadow of the largest palm by the windows, Travis watched her for a moment, envying her the tranquil nature of her dreams as much as her ability to sleep before he turned to stare blindly into the night.

What, he wondered tensely, was he going to do about Alex?

He shifted, bracing a hand against the window frame, his gaze passing restlessly over the lawn and gardens below. It was a beautiful night, with only a slight breeze to rustle the trees. High overhead, a milky three-quarter moon hung in a dark blue sky strewn with pale yellow stars, to which he blindly lifted his eyes, his thoughts disturbed.

I can't abide lying. Alex's words played through his mind. It'd been bad enough when all he was doing was abusing her hospitality. But now, knowing how she felt about lying—and liars—it was far worse, and he didn't like the way he was feeling. It was almost as if he cared.

And as much as it disturbed him to have to deceive her, the idea that he was coming to care for her was even more disturbing. In the course of a day, everything—and nothing—had changed, and he didn't like the unaccustomed feeling surging to life inside him.

He was thirty-four years old, and for more than twenty years the cardinal rule of his life had been *Don't get involved.* Involvement meant setting yourself up for pain and abandonment, leaving yourself wide open to false hopes, betting on a future that never worked out the way you planned.

Staying apart, on the other hand, kept those sort of demons at bay. Avoiding entanglements had even given him an edge in his job, since there was no reason to hang back when you had nothing to lose and nobody to give a damn, anyway.

All in all, he thought it was a pretty good rule to live by; God knows, the rare times he *hadn't* followed it had sure as hell ended in disaster.

There was the affair with Beth, of course, although recently he'd been thinking about it and was willing to concede that the problem there could have been his insistence on keeping his inner self apart, as opposed to their actually getting involved. Beth had certainly thought so.

But as to the other time he'd let down his guard, he had no such doubt. He'd opened himself up, he'd allowed himself to care—and it had blown up in his face.

Damn you, Joel, he thought now, his hand fisting against the windowsill. *Why did you have to presume on our friendship and ask me for that particular assignment? And why the hell couldn't you have been more careful for once?*

I told you I had a bad feeling about LeClair. Why didn't you listen when you called and I told you to stay put? Why didn't you wait for me? Why did you have to go and get yourself killed?

But even as the anguished questions rolled through his mind, he knew from grim experience the futility of such thinking.

Joel was gone; Travis had had his time of rage and grief, and about the only good thing that could be said was that lately the crushing emptiness that had come in their wake had begun to diminish a bit. Other than that, he took solace in that he was doing the best he could to see that the person responsible paid, which was really the only thing left for him to do.

But of course that brought him back to Alex.

What the hell should he do?

He smiled in self-deprecation, allowing as how the question might be rhetorical at this point, kind of like wondering whether or not to fix a broken fence when the horse was already well on its way down the road.

So okay, he and Alex had had sex; well, maybe not just sex. They'd had great sex, world-class sex, the best-he'd-ever-had sex, and like a kid with his first taste of sugar, he wasn't ready to give it up.

That didn't mean he cared.

So what if she was beautiful and witty, and as welcoming as a crackling fire on a cold winter's day? So what if the generous way she offered herself to him—open and trusting, with nothing held back—made him feel a thousand feet tall? So what if with a few droll little words she could nearly always make him smile?

In a few more days Mac should be back and, fabulous sex or not, he'd be on his way.

So why was he worrying?

It wasn't as if he'd made any promises. As a matter of fact, he'd been damn straight, making sure before they ever got involved that Alex knew he planned to leave.

Involved. There was that word again. Maybe that was what was eating at him, and not the sinking feeling he had in his gut that if Alex ever found out the whole story—that he'd been lying when he told her he was retiring, that he was using her house as a base for his cat-and-mouse game with LeClair—she'd see it as a violation of her trust, and be hurt.

For all that he didn't care about her, something inside him shied away at the thought of causing her pain. She deserved better; at the very least, to be cherished and protected. At the most, she deserved to be loved—or would, he amended, rejecting the thought as swiftly as it had come, if he believed in that sort of thing.

But still... the idea lingered. It was that air of peacefulness about her, an inherent gentleness in her nature that put him in mind of such things, making him ache for the dreams he'd put aside years ago.

Outside the window, a streak of light caught his eye as a solitary star shot across the sky, the last spectacular flight of a distant sun. In mere seconds, it was gone, with nothing to mark its passage. And yet, he thought slowly, that wasn't precisely true. For it would live in his memory, gaining a sort of eternity in his appreciation of its brief but splendid beauty. And for some inexplicable reason, he found the idea comforting.

In the bed, Alex stirred, then called softly, her voice heavy with sleep, "Travis?"

With one long last look at the sky, he turned and made his way back to the bed, slipping into the waiting warmth of Alex's arms. "Mmm," she said drowsily, her arms twining around his neck, her lips soft as they found the hollow in the base of his throat. "Much better."

Passion leapt to life instantly at her words, but even as it claimed him and he returned her embrace, rolling her beneath him, a single thought continued to torment him.

What am I going to do about Alex?

What am I going to do about Travis?

Alex scrubbed at the spotless kitchen countertop the next morning, trying to put an answer to the question she'd been asking herself since dawn, when she'd slipped quietly out of a sleeping Travis's arms.

So much had happened in the past twenty-four hours. Had it been only yesterday that she realized her feelings for Travis? Since then, so much had changed. *She* had changed.

Ever since Stefan had died, she'd refused to acknowledge her need for someone with whom to share her life, she realized, telling herself she had no need for a man or children of her own. She'd convinced herself she was fulfilled with her life as it was. She'd been a good friend, a sterling neighbor, the best courtesy aunt a child could want, but she'd been careful not to become the main focus or support of anyone's life. What if she failed them? What if she made a mistake?

What if they died?

She paused in her scrubbing, staring blankly out the kitchen window, finally admitting that was the crux of the problem. When she'd awakened this morning, it had all seemed so clear; she, who had prided herself on the way she'd gone on after Stefan's death, had only been fooling herself.

Oh, she'd done all the right things. She'd faced off the press, so calm and dignified in her grief they'd quickly abandoned her for more spectacular news. She'd quietly sold off Stefan's holdings, putting the bulk of his money in a trust that benefited a multitude of good causes and charities, taking only a modest amount for herself, eschewing a more glamorous life-style. Like a good little girl, she'd studied for her master's degree, she'd landed a job, she'd bought her house. She'd carved out a life for herself, filling it with work and friends, telling herself that was enough.

She was comfortable with her solidly middle-class background, and her only extravagance had been the Ferrari; she could see now that the sleek, fast car had been the only outward expression of the passionate side of her nature she'd allowed herself.

And then Travis had literally burst into her life.

Although it might appear that circumstance had forced them together, Alex knew it wasn't really true. She hadn't had to bring him home with her that first day, and she could have found a solution other than her taking care of him when he got the chicken pox.

But from the first moment he vaulted into her car, her attraction to him had been stronger than her fears, more compelling than all the if-onlys that she now realized had been haunting her since Stefan's death.

If only they had chosen a different place to honeymoon. If only she'd been content to drink tea and hadn't wanted coffee. If only she'd demanded they go the few extra blocks to the grocery story. If only she'd insisted on going into the convenience store alone, if only she'd crossed the threshold first, if only they hadn't walked in on that robbery, if only she'd reacted faster. If, if, if—and none of it mattered, because nothing would ever bring her husband back.

She shuddered, remembering Stefan's face, and the blood that had covered everything. . . .

But it was over now. Still, she couldn't help but be grateful Travis was leaving the State Department. Although she refused to allow herself to think that something permanent might come out of their temporary affair, the thought of him facing danger day in and day out made her blood run cold. She would sleep better at night knowing he was safe.

Which didn't answer her question about what she should do about Travis. Should she tell him she loved him? She'd been debating with herself for hours. While on the one hand she wanted to tell him, feeling he deserved to know that he was loved, that he had a special place in her heart and always would, on the other she was afraid the knowledge might do more harm than good.

She didn't want him to feel obligated. She'd gone into this with her eyes open; he'd been very careful to spell out his beliefs and expectations—or lack of them—and she didn't want to cause him distress with a declaration.

There was also the chance such an announcement might send him running for the hills, and she didn't want to cut short even a second of their already limited time together. And then there was—

"Good morning."

The deep, quiet voice put an end to Alex's jumbled thoughts. Her eyes jerked to the doorway, where Travis stood, wearing nothing more than a pair of low-slung jeans. "Hi," she responded, feeling self-conscious as his gaze played over her. Certain that what she felt for him must be written all over her face, she nervously scooped up a handful of silverware and hurried to the table, where the place mats and napkins were already laid out.

"Are you hungry? Do you want to have breakfast now? Or do you want to shower first?" She knew she was babbling, but she couldn't seem to stop. "I thought maybe you might want to go to the mall with me later. I need some—"

"Alex." His quiet voice cut her off.

Already busy setting the table, she tensed. "What?"

"Can I have a cup of coffee?"

She froze, a fork clutched in her hand, sending him a stricken look while privately thinking it unfair that he should affect her so strongly simply because he was bare-chested and his hair was sexily tousled. "Oh, of course. I'm sorry, I'll—"

"I can get it," he said, pushing off from the door frame and approaching the coffeepot. Taking a cup out of the cabinet, he poured himself some of the rich, hot brew, then turned and leaned against the counter, the white tile floor cool beneath his bare feet. He blew on his coffee and took a sip, regarding Alex over the rim of the cup.

She'd already showered; her hair was neatly braided, and she was dressed in a pale blue blouse and crisp white slacks. She looked elegant and untouchable; only a closer look revealed the faint tremor in her hands, the slight shadows beneath her eyes, the bee-stung appearance of her lips. He couldn't deny the primitive satisfaction that blazed to life inside him at the visual proof of how thoroughly he'd made love to her.

She looked up, her gaze wary, almost shy. "So? Do you want to eat now?" she asked in that overly bright tone that was rapidly getting on his nerves.

Wondering what the hell was wrong, he ran a hand through his disordered hair and gave a shrug, then crossed to the table. "Sure. Might as well." He seated himself, then did a double take at the food piled there—sausage, bacon and ham, baked eggs, hash browns, toast, pancakes, syrup and jam, and a beaker of melted butter—and all of it in quantities generous enough to feed a Third World country.

This from a woman whose normal version of breakfast was low-fat yogurt or granola with skim milk? A woman who'd informed him four days ago when he'd wanted a doughnut and coffee for breakfast that she refused to contribute to the hardening of his arteries? Who condemned chicken noodle soup as a health hazard in a can?

He laid down his fork with a decisive click, the sound of the silverware meeting the china shattering the quiet like a pistol shot. His blue eyes bore into her. "What's the matter?" His gaze probed Alex's pale face, his stomach plummeting as the obvious answer to his question occurred to him. "Have you finally realized that sleeping with me was a big mistake?"

For a second, Alex's eyes rounded in surprise, then her face cleared and she sank into the chair to his right, reaching across the narrow space separating them to lay her hand against his cheek. "No, that's not it at all," she said gently. "I'm behaving badly because—" she took a deep breath "—I love you, and I was trying to figure out whether or not to tell you."

Travis stared at her, feeling stunned and wondering why. Alex was a class act; he'd known from the moment he met her she wasn't the kind of woman to sleep around, a conviction more than confirmed by the reaction of her neighbors yesterday, not to mention the information Brandon so freely handed out. Hadn't he known, in some dark corner of his brain, that she wasn't the kind of woman to be so free with herself, so generous, so giving, unless she really cared?

So why was he sitting here staring at her with all the savoir faire of a beached trout? Was it because he didn't know what to say? Or was it because he was secretly relieved? That even though he didn't reciprocate, even though he'd deny it with his last breath, there was a part of him that had desperately needed to hear her say those three little words?

Pressing her hand to his face with his own, he marveled at the delicacy of her slender fingers, the narrowness of her palm. "Why were you afraid?" he asked finally.

Her brows rose fractionally as if she wondered that he had to ask. "I know how you feel about love. I didn't want you to feel crowded or...obligated. I didn't want you to leave."

He digested that. "So what made you decide to tell me?" he asked.

She shrugged, a delicate ripple of her slender shoulders. "What else could I do? Stand by and keep silent while you thought the worst?" Turning her wrist, she entwined her fingers with his much longer, stronger ones and gave them a squeeze. "I couldn't let you think what you were thinking just because I was afraid to tell you the truth."

Her words struck him like a blow. She was doing it again, he realized, turning him upside down and inside out. It made him feel on top of the world to hear her say she loved him—and like a first-class heel to realize she was willing to risk rejection and possible hurt for herself in order to spare his feelings. "Alex, don't..." he said hoarsely, only to stop as he had no idea how to go on. Should he tell her? Tell her he'd lied to her, that he wasn't really retired, that even though he didn't mean to, he'd been using her, using her house?

She sighed, then gave him a smile that was sweetness itself. "Shh," she said, bringing his hand to her face and rubbing the back of it against her cheek. "There's no need to say anything. That was one of the reasons I wasn't sure I should tell you, because I was afraid you'd feel like you had to say something in return, and I didn't want that. So let it go, okay?

"Besides—" her eyes suddenly sparked with mischief as she brought one of his fingers to her mouth and gave it a playful nip "—I already know your deep dark secret. I finally put the pieces together this morning. Why didn't you tell me?"

Fear slammed into him as he instantly assumed the worst, and he spat a colorful Anglo-Saxon expletive through his teeth that brought a rush of color to her face. "Travis!" she exclaimed.

Even as relief poured through him—she knew the worst and still seemed to care—he grabbed her hand in a grip so tight it hurt. "What happened?" he demanded, cursing himself roundly for exposing her to danger. Damn it, he'd been so careful! "Did somebody call here? What did the bastard say?" How the hell had LeClair gotten her number, anyway? Shoving back his chair, he stood and started to pace, needing some outlet for the agitation the thought of any harm coming to Alex brought him.

Alex watched in amazement as he stalked around the kitchen with all the ill temper of a caged panther. When she'd awakened this morning, out of the blue had come the certain knowledge that the name of the author of *The Great Beyond* wasn't Tracks, but Trax—which was how Travis signed himself: *T, R, A* and *X* for Cross. And just like that, she'd known. She'd been charmed, surprised—and fallen even more in love with him at the realization that no matter how much he denied it, the sensitive, optimistic side of him had survived his lonely childhood despite everything to live in his book.

Never had she imagined he'd have such a violent reaction to being discovered. If she had, she would never have said a word. "Travis, relax. If you don't want it known you're the mind behind Milton Monster, just say so. Your secret's safe with me."

Pacing away, he froze in midstride and rounded on her. "What?"

"I won't tell anyone Milton's your monster, I swear."

"You know about Milton, too?" he said incredulously.

She frowned as the tension that had been holding him taut disappeared. "Am I missing something here?" she inquired, looking at him expectantly. "What do you mean, 'too'? I know about Milton, period."

It was the perfect opening. *Tell her,* Travis's conscience screamed. *Tell her all of it.*

But what if she despised him for lying? What if she quit looking at him with that incredible tenderness? What if she turned her back on him the way his mother had?

And what if she kicked him out? Like it or not, he had a job to do. Mac should be back any day now, and with luck, they'd have the evidence to put the kibosh on LeClair once and for all. It would be damned irresponsible to do anything to screw it up now.

Still. What the hell did he say to Alex?

Unwittingly, she herself provided him with an out. "Have you written another book, a different book, too?"

Hadn't he decided that what Alex didn't know couldn't hurt her? Better that *he* hate himself for being a total jerk rather than take a chance of Alex's getting hurt. Besides, business came first, he reminded himself. He had a job to do, and by God he was going to do it. "Yes," he said, slowly moving back toward the table and sitting down. He picked up a piece of bacon and bit off a healthy chunk, and for the first time it occurred to him to wonder how she'd learned about his connection to *The Great Beyond.*

Heaping food on his plate, he asked and she explained concluding, "...it was your signature on the Sasquatch that gave you away. But tell me about your new book. Is it about Milton, too?"

"It was," he said, finding a surprising amount of comfort in sharing the confidence. "It's gone."

"Gone?"

"With my luggage." Whether his bags had been lost by the airline or fraudulently claimed with the baggage stubs that had been in his stolen wallet, his luggage had never turned up. "The script and the final sketches were inside. I'd planned to do some polishing and send it on to my editor while I was here. But now..." He shrugged.

Despite his nonchalant expression, Alex could see how troubled he was. "Oh, Travis. All that work..." she said with genuine regret. And before he could head her off, she closed the distance between them and gave him a sympathetic hug. "I'm so sorry. But maybe your stuff will turn up yet. And if not, surely you can redo it?"

Yeah, right. Just as soon as he got out of therapy for the guilt complex she was giving him. Unless, of course, he died first from terminal lust, he amended, nuzzling her with his mouth as she cradled his head against her breasts. He took a deep breath, thinking to get his unruly thoughts under control, but that was a big mistake, too. She smelled like sunshine and flowers, with a faintly exotic scent all of her own that had that extraordinary effect on his libido.

Surrendering to temptation, he wound his arms around her waist and hauled her onto his lap.

"Travis!" she protested, even as she snuggled closer.

"Alex," he mimicked in a husky falsetto, just before he tasted the smooth skin of her neck.

"I thought we were going to the mall...."

"Later," he said, nibbling on her ear. "But first I think we'll make a little detour...upstairs."

"Oh..." she said breathlessly.

It was the last word she uttered for quite a while.

Ten

———

The phone pressed to his ear, Travis waited impatiently for the tinny-voiced receptionist at State to answer the phone, but it wasn't until the eighth ring that he heard the nasal drawl he'd come to despise say, "State Department. How may I help you?"

"Travis Cross for Derwin MacGregor," he said, just as he had all the other times he'd called in the past three days. He braced himself for her usual gleeful retort that Mac still wasn't in.

Instead, she said briskly, "One moment, please. I'll ring Mr. MacGregor's office for you."

There were a series of clicks and whirs, and in seconds another voice came on the line. "MacGregor," it barked.

"Cross," Travis barked back.

"Hey, boyo, great timing!" The bureau chief's smile could be heard in his voice. "Where are you? When I got in last night I called the hotel and gave your cover name, and they said they'd never heard of you. I was worried. Everything all right?''

"I had a few problems in the beginning, but you can read about that in my report," Travis said, neatly sidestepping the question regarding his location. "The important thing is, what did you find out?"

"LeClair's accountant rolled over like a greased log and gave us everything but his socks," Mac said gleefully, his satisfaction audible.

"Thank God." Travis felt like a weight had been lifted from his shoulders, and yet the savage satisfaction he'd expected to feel when this moment came never materialized. Instead, he felt a quiet sort of completion, pleasant to be sure, but nothing like what he'd anticipated. Listening as Mac went on, he puzzled over the unexpected flatness of his reaction.

"Bless his weasely little heart, Michaels—that's the accountant—even kept a copy of the books, the *real* books. Seems LeClair has this thing for writing everything down— he even had Michaels break out the expenses for the kidnapping." MacGregor paused and his voice lost all traces of joviality. "You realize, don't you, Cross, that we probably won't be able to take LeClair down on either the Rackowzi boy's kidnapping or Joel's murder? It's the tax-evasion charges that are going to put him away."

It was a hell of a long way from Travis's solution of choice—but then, the government tended to frown on death by dismemberment. And yet oddly enough, Travis realized slowly, the news didn't make him feel angry or bitter the way it would have a month ago. For the first time since he'd found Joel's lifeless body, what was important was LeClair be punished—however it was accomplished.

He sensed that Mac was waiting breathlessly, bracing for an explosion.

With a slight, sardonic smile at the bureau chief's assessment of his character, he said mildly, "Well, boss, if that's the only way we can do it, let's go for it."

There was dead silence and then a rusty chuckle. "Damn you, Cross. You never act the way I expect you to."

"Yeah, well—that's part of my charm."

Mac made a decidedly rude sound, and then he sighed and said seriously, sounding tired, "I don't know, boyo. Sometimes I think we work for the wrong arm of the government. It seems like these days you can get away with kidnapping a foreign national or ordering the death of a federal agent—but nobody escapes the long arm of the IRS."

"Yeah, I guess," Travis said half-heartedly. He looked around Alex's cheerful kitchen with its profusion of plants and its sun-splattered walls, and he experienced a sudden letdown of his own and an unexpected—and totally unacceptable—sense of loss.

He scowled at the unwanted emotion, telling himself sternly it was all a matter of interior decorating as a picture of his house in Connecticut flashed into his mind. He wouldn't be feeling this way if he'd ever bothered to furnish it. The thought of returning to nothing but a bed, a card table, three folding chairs and one oversize brass hat rack after the pleasant comfort of Alex's house was enough to depress anybody.

"Hey, Cross, are you there?"

Travis brought his wandering attention back to the phone, thankful for the diversion. "Yeah, Mac, I'm here. So when do we move?"

"I'm meeting with the IRS guys in about a half an hour, and we should have the indictment and a warrant some time this afternoon. Can you arrange a meeting with LeClair for tomorrow?"

Tomorrow. Typical, Travis thought. The arraignment was supposed to be tomorrow. Nothing for weeks, and then everything all at once. "No problem. The bastard's so hot to get the diamonds back you can practically hear him salivating on the other end of the phone."

"Okay. So why don't you give me your number, and I'll call you in the morning when I get into town."

Realizing there was no other way, Travis reluctantly complied. "But Mac—don't give it to anyone else," he cautioned. "I'm staying with a... friend, and I don't want her put in any danger, you understand?"

MacGregor didn't have any compunctions against prying. "A friend, huh? Somebody special?"

Travis didn't want to discuss Alex. "Naw, just a friend," he lied. "She'll be glad to see the last of me, and it's past time for me to go."

But Mac wasn't buying it. "Yeah, right. How many years have I known you? Ten? Twelve? You don't have 'friends.' This must be some broad, huh?" His tone was knowing. But when it was met with a heavy, total silence, he quickly took the hint and changed the subject. "Yeah, well..." He cleared his throat. "Have you talked to Stella, by chance?"

At the reference to Mac's superefficient secretary, Travis grew puzzled. "No. I thought she was with you."

"Naw. I can't figure it out. She left word she'd had a family crisis, but I called her sister who says she hasn't heard from her. I'm worried—she hasn't been herself the past few months...." A reluctant suspicion was in his voice.

"Hell. Are you thinking what I think you are?"

"Yeah, but I sure hope I'm wrong— Damn, there goes my other line. Gotta run, boyo. I'll call you first thing tomorrow. In the meantime, don't do anything I wouldn't do."

"Well, that leaves it wide open," Travis said dryly. "You gonna post my bail?"

Mac made a suggestion that was not only rude, but probably physically impossible, as well.

With a low chuckle, Travis responded in kind and hung up.

Staring into space, Travis automatically rocked the porch swing, wondering at the somber mood that had descended on him since he'd talked to Mac.

Brandon, who was perched at his side, looked at him uncertainly. "You look like a blunder cloud."

"Yeah, well," Travis muttered, reflecting that the kid had inadvertently gotten it right. Still, he forced his face into what he hoped were less-severe lines. "Relax. I promise not to bite."

The little boy thought about that for a minute before saying, "'Kay."

Silence descended once again, the only sound the faint creak of the swing, which Travis restlessly continued to push back and forth. Finally Brandon ventured to ask, "Are you mad at Auntie Alex?"

Travis turned to stare at him in surprise. "Whatever gave you that idea?"

Brandon shrugged, pulling a fat purple marker from his pants pocket. Idly picking at a tiny tear in the thigh of his jeans, he uncapped the felt pen and began to color his newly exposed skin. "I heard my mom and dad talking," he confided, glancing briefly off in the direction of a neighbor's yard when a dog barked.

Travis could hardly wait to hear this. "You did?"

Brandon's head bobbed. "Yeah. My mom said you were mad about Auntie Alex. She said she could see it in your eyes." He abandoned his coloring project to twist on the seat and stare earnestly into Travis's eyes. After several seconds he sank back down and shook his head decisively. "Nope. I don't see anything in there."

Out of the mouths of babes, Travis thought, and despite his bleak mood, a wry inner smile touched his lips. Squinting against the glare of the sun, he took his sunglasses from his shirt pocket and slipped them on. "I'm not angry with Alex. Being mad *about* somebody is different from being mad *at* them—when you're mad *about* them, it means you like them a lot."

"Oh." Brandon gave the tear in his pants a jerk with his index finger, enlarging it considerably, and began to color a fresh section of skin as he pondered that. "Mommy told Daddy that Auntie Alex *loves* you." He stressed the word, then looked up at Travis expectantly.

Not for the first time, Travis wished Brad and Sarah Nelson wouldn't talk so openly where their son could overhear. Still, it wasn't in him to lie to Brandon. "Yeah. I guess she does."

Brandon stared with seeming fascination at his bright purple skin. "So why don't you love her back? Auntie Alex is *rad.*"

"Yeah, she is," Travis said, and he meant it. "But you see, buddy," he began, trying to frame his emotions in a way the child could understand, "love isn't for everybody. You know how smart your mom is? Well, my mom wasn't quite so smart as yours. My dad died when I was even younger than Lizabeth is now, and my mom wanted a husband real bad, so she got married again. When it didn't work, she tried again. So instead of being married once or even twice, she tried it lots of times...."

"But that's okay," Brandon pointed out. "That's like what you said at practice."

Travis's eyes narrowed behind his darkly tinted glasses. "What did I say at practice?"

"You said even if you strike out, or miss the ball, what's important is not to give up."

"Well, maybe I did, but—"

"Maybe your mom was lonesome. I know my mom gets lonesome for my dad when he's gone—even though she has me and pesky old Lizabeth."

It was a shock, but Travis realized he'd never thought of his mother simply as a woman who might have been lonely when her husband died. She'd failed *him* as a parent, and that disappointment had blinded him to the fact that she was still a person, with frailties and needs of her own.

Brandon reached over and took his hand, the fact that his small fingers were unable to close around Travis's broad palm in no way diminishing the comfort the gesture meant. "At least she tried," Brandon pointed out with inescapable logic. "You said it didn't matter if Sean's brother was a big star on the junior-high team—it was what Sean did that was important. That was cool, 'cuz Sean's always acting like he's real rad just because of Ronnie, who's an even bigger jerk than he is, but..." His voice faltered for the first time, as a new thought occurred to him. "Didn't you mean it? Or is that one of those things grown-ups say that's only for kids?"

Travis pulled off his sunglasses and rubbed at his eyes with his thumb and index finger, feeling a little like he'd just been struck by a bus. "No," he said slowly, "it's not. Or at least, it shouldn't be." Lowering his hand, he glanced over to find Brandon squinting at him worriedly, a V of concern etched between his brows.

Impulsively he reached out and settled his sunglasses on the boy's pert nose. "You've got a great career ahead of you in diplomacy, kid. A memory like an elephant and the persistence of a mule will shoot you right to the top."

Even though he didn't know what diplomacy was, Brandon responded to the wry curve of Travis's mouth with a charmingly lopsided grin of his own that made the glasses slide off his nose. Then, as if giving a demonstration of the persistence Travis had mentioned, he cocked his head and said, "So? Now do you love Auntie Alex?"

Travis's eyes darkened, desire and something bordering on tenderness filling him as he thought about Alex's gentle teasing, the softness in her eyes when she looked at him, the unreserved way she gave herself to him in bed, the generosity she'd shown in sharing her friends and opening her life to him. He thought of how she'd taken him in when he was sick, the humor and compassion with which she'd bullied him into doing what was best, her uncritical acceptance of who and what he was.

Still, the warmth he felt when he thought about her wasn't love. He didn't believe in love.

Impatient with his silence, Brandon sighed. "I don't get it. Grown-ups are so stoo-pid sometimes."

"You've got that right," said a soft, feminine voice that had both males swiveling their heads to the right, where Alex stood at the corner of the porch. With a faint smile, she came and sat down beside Brandon.

Travis wondered how long she'd been standing there, how much she'd overheard. Of course, given Brandon's penchant for repeating everything said to him, she'd probably have a verbatim report of their entire conversation soon enough, anyway.

He cleared his throat. "How was your day?" he asked, his eyes sliding appreciatively over her navy linen suit. She looked cool and professional in the classically cut style with her navy spectator pumps.

"Fine," Alex said, groaning with relief as she slid off her high heels, "although I'm not sure there's any hope for my freshman class. They speak English as if *it* were a foreign language." Resting her head against the swing back, she stretched and crossed one leg over the other, sending her short skirt sliding up her thighs, exposing one lace-edged snap of her garter belt. Out of the corner of her eye she caught Travis staring with rapt appreciation at the lace rosette. Smiling with inner satisfaction as a faint flush crept up his neck, she smoothed her skirt down. Slowly. "How about you?"

"Okay." He'd tell her later that he'd started rewriting the sequel to *The Great Beyond*. Hell. He hadn't anything better to do, and it beat sitting around and brooding.

"Guess what, Auntie Alex!" Brandon interjected. "I got a new pair of baseball shoes. They've got creeps. Rubber ones. I'll really be able to run when we play the Mighty Mouses Saturday."

"Bran, I think you mean cleats," Alex corrected gently.

"That's what I said. With Travis helping we're gonna beat those dirty rat Mouses, aren't we, Auntie Alex?"

"Absolutely."

Travis cleared his throat, and although his words were addressed to Brandon, his gaze was on Alex. "I'm sorry, buddy, but you're going to have to do this one on your own. I won't be here Saturday."

Alex's smile froze, and she could actually feel the blood drain from her face. With an effort of will, she forced her voice to stay even. "What about the trial?" she asked lightly.

"Everything'll be wrapped up tomorrow," he said, skirting the issue.

Alex didn't pursue it. She didn't want details; she wanted to escape, desperately needing time to get herself under control so she could maintain her seeming serenity. It had been hard enough when she'd overheard Travis's telling silence when Brandon asked if he loved her. But now, as she was actually confronted with the fact of his leaving, pain knifed through her.

"But I don't want you to go!" Brandon wailed, inadvertently echoing the cry in her own heart.

Travis tore his eyes away from Alex's white face and forced himself to concentrate on Brandon. *She knew I was going,* he thought fiercely. *I never promised her anything.*

"I know, bud. But this isn't my home. I've just been visiting. You know that." Again, although the words were directed at the child, they were meant for Alex.

You knew he was going, Alex reminded herself brutally. He'd never pretended, never made any empty promises. *Don't ruin the time you have left with what-ifs and could-have-beens.*

Taking a deep, steadying breath, she managed to say with credible calmness, "Travis's right, Bran." She gave the child's knee a commiserating pat. "And even though we'll miss Travis, we'll survive. Why, with what he taught you guys, I bet we win."

Over the boy's head, Alex's open golden gaze met Travis's shuttered blue one. They exchanged a long look, filled on both sides with silent questions for which there appeared to be no satisfactory answers.

And when they finally managed to look away, it was hard to say who was more shaken.

They went out to dinner that night at a small Italian restaurant near the mall. They discussed politics and religion, Alex's job and Travis's college experience in Europe. Alex told him about her childhood in northern Idaho; he told her how he'd created Milton during a stakeout to counteract the boredom of endless hours of waiting, explaining how it had been his friend Joel who'd actually sent the finished product to a publisher. The editor's enthusiastic reply—and subsequent offer of a three-book contract—had taken him by surprise.

Alex refrained from pointing out that as a writer, he could work—and live—anywhere.

Her restraint was indicative of the atmosphere of the meal, which was pleasant if slightly strained, as they continued to chat amiably but meaninglessly, scrupulously avoiding the one thing most on both their minds—Travis's coming departure.

It wasn't until they were back at Alex's house and crossing the threshold into the bedroom that their respective facades shattered. Faced with the prospect of what might very well be their last night together, Alex's composure snapped and she turned to him, no longer entirely able to disguise her despair. She wound her arms around his neck, pressing him to her heart, her mouth seeking his with desperate need. "Make love to me," she said urgently. They only had tonight, and she wanted him so.

Already he was so hard he hurt. He couldn't recall ever feeling like this, as if he'd explode if he couldn't be inside her. He met the tantalizing motions she was making against his body with a desperation of his own.

She kissed him, her mouth hot and insistent. "I need you."

"We have tonight," he murmured, closing his eyes against the inexplicable pain of his own words. It wasn't enough, but it was the best he could do.

He broke the kiss only long enough for them to undress, then he drew her into his arms, falling back against the mattress, pulling her down on top of him. His mouth drifted over the sensitive flesh behind her ear. "You taste like honey," he said fiercely, as she pressed feverish little kisses along the hard line of his jaw. Her naked body felt like cool silk against his aching, overheated flesh. Hungrily seeking her mouth, he threaded one of his hands into her hair, the other finding her delicate palm and engulfing it with his.

Alex gave a little gasp as he pulled her higher up on his chest, his eyes hot with appreciation as he looked up at her. "The night I met you," he said huskily, "when I first saw this room, I imagined myself here, with you, like this." He tugged her head down, nipping at her lower lip, then nuzzled the satiny skin at the base of her cheek.

With a soft exclamation, she molded herself against him like a second skin, her hands stroking restlessly over the contours of his upper body. "I love you, Travis." She could no longer restrain the words that spilled from her heart as the tips of her fingers tenderly roved over the taut muscle of his chest, then explored the smooth expanse of his broad back.

She rocked back, rising up to straddle his waist. Her hands mapped his torso before coming to rest at his lean waist. With eyes full of discovery she stroked him, feeling a growing excitement at the primitive satisfaction so openly displayed on his face.

His hands reached up to cup her breasts. "So pretty," he murmured huskily.

Alex flushed a soft shade of pink. "Travis..."

"I want to be buried deep inside you, Alex. I want to feel your hair slide across my chest. I want to feel your nipples in my mouth..."

She moaned, the sound drawn from deep inside her. Her body stiffened, her hands clutched his shoulders. Shivers of delight rippled down her spine. Her breasts were so sensitive that when he drew her down and his tongue swirled around one tight tip, she could actually feel the heat pooling in the center of her body. She rocked against him in an instinctual urge to assuage that heated ache.

Travis groaned low in his throat. "Easy, lady. Take it slow," he rasped, trying to calm them both. His hands shaped her from neck to breast, lingering over the smallness of her waist, the fullness of her hips, then moving lower to rest at last on the soft curls at the notch of her thighs.

She shivered, waves of pleasure buffeting her.

"So damn soft," Travis murmured. With gentle fingers he touched her, until her head was turning from side to side as the pad of his thumb circled the silky, demanding core of her.

Alex felt as if she were standing high on a precipice and the slightest movement would send her plunging over the edge in a free-fall. "Please," she gasped.

His own breathing labored, Travis complied, his heart nearly leaping out of his chest at the overwhelming pleasure as they were joined.

"Alex." He touched her cheek, holding himself still inside her. "Look at me." She opened glazed eyes to stare down at him in wonder. His face was hard with desire, his gaze searing in its intensity.

Holding his eyes with her own, she began to move, pulling away and returning, giving herself, until he was once again deep inside her. With slow, measured strokes she loved him, until he was twisting helplessly, arching off the bed to meet her.

And still she worshiped him with her hands, her body, her mouth. Time and time again she brought them to the brink of fulfillment, only to stop and begin anew, drawing it out, making each second count, until at the end, nothing mattered, nothing existed except each for the other and the miracle of being one.

And when it was over, long after Travis had finally fallen into an exhausted sleep, Alex lay staring blindly into the night, buffeted by wave after wave of desolation at the crushing realization of how much she would miss him.

Choking back tears, her head nestled in the curve of his arm, she listened to the steady beat of his heart, finding a strange sort of comfort in the strong, slow sound.

At least, she thought, stroking her hand tenderly over his warm, solid body, I'll always have tonight.

It would have to be enough.

Eleven

———

The ringing of the phone woke Alex well before dawn.

Groggily handing the receiver to Travis, she listened as he held a brief, monosyllabic conversation she was too sleepy to follow. Assuming the call had something to do with the arraignment, when he asked if he could borrow her car she mumbled that would be fine and drifted back to sleep.

When she awoke hours later, he was gone.

Realizing as soon as the first wave of panic abated that he wasn't gone for good—yet—she tried to think about the day ahead, but her heart wasn't in it. Instead, as she lay in bed and looked at the sea of clouds beyond her windows, she decided she felt the way the day looked. Overcast.

She couldn't believe he was really going to go.

But he was. Sometime in the next twenty-four hours he would get on an airplane and fly away.

It was not, Alex told herself, the end of the world. She'd be all right. Oh, it might be painful for a while, but in a few weeks or months—or years—the anguish of separation would fade and she would be able to look back on her spring fling with a fond but worldly smile.

Right, said the little voice in her head. Is that the same day pigs are going to fly? The day Brandon is going to stop asking questions? The day DeeDee gives up men?

She had a sudden urge to cry.

Staunchly forcing away the surge of self-pity, she crawled out of bed and pulled on her oldest jeans and a *U* of *W* sweatshirt with the arms ripped out, and proceeded to attack her house, starting with fresh sheets on the bed and moving on to vacuum, scrub and dust. By eleven the entire place was so clean it sparkled, and she was just finishing folding the last of Travis's freshly laundered clothes. Placing a T-shirt on the meager stack of items on top of the dryer, she couldn't stop herself from reaching out and caressing the smooth cotton, her hands tenderly smoothing away a nonexistent wrinkle. Only the ringing of the phone saved her from becoming maudlin.

She hurried into the kitchen and grabbed the receiver, grateful for the interruption, thinking it might be Travis. "Hello?"

It wasn't. "Alex? Hi, it's Sarah. How are you?"

She knew instantly from her friend's overly solicitous tone that Brandon had reported Travis was leaving. "I'm fine. Travis had some business in Seattle, so I'm catching up on my chores."

Sarah's tone was painfully sympathetic. "The hunk is really leaving, huh?"

"Yes," Alex said with a brightness that was as phony as a three-dollar bill. "Later today, probably."

Sarah didn't buy it for a minute. "Listen, Alex, did it ever occur to you to ask him to stay? Anybody with half a brain can see he's crazy about you."

"Sarah—"

The other woman cut across her protest. "Tell him he's ruined you for other men. Tell him it's cruel of him to leave you with your engine running and nowhere to go. Tell him something, for heaven's sake. But don't stand silently by and let him go. Being a martyr isn't going to keep you warm at night."

Alex knew Sarah meant well, but maintaining her equilibrium was hard enough without Sarah inciting her to leap over the edge. "Is that all you called to say? Because if it is, I have things to do—"

"Just think about it, okay?"

As if she hadn't.

"Promise?"

"Fine," Alex said shortly.

Sarah knew to quit when she was ahead. "Listen, I hate to do this, especially with everything else you have going on, but I have a favor to ask. Would you mind watching Brandon and Lizabeth for about an hour? I need to drop by the cleaners and then see if I can find some shoes for that office party Brad and I are going to."

"Sure," Alex said instantly, welcoming the diversion. Keeping up with Brandon and Lizabeth would definitely prevent her from getting overly sentimental. "Do you want me to come there or do you want to leave them here?"

"Bless you," Sarah said with a thankful sigh, "but don't even think of coming over." She gave a little laugh. "I don't want to take any chances on your changing your mind, and one look at my house, which currently looks like it was struck by a tornado, would be enough to give anybody second thoughts. I'll be there as soon as Brandon gets off the kindergarten bus."

"Okay. See you then."

Alex spent the next half hour making a double batch of brownies. A little while later, there was a swift knock on the front door, and Sarah and the two little Nelsons came trooping in. "Hi," Alex said brightly.

"You won't be so cheerful by the time I get back," Sarah assured her, letting go of Brandon's hand and lowering Lizabeth to the floor.

"That bad, huh?" Alex said, as Brandon raced down the hall doing an imitation of a dive-bomber. Arms outstretched, he swooped around the corner and dove into the kitchen, apparently following the scent of the brownies cooling on the counter. Lizabeth toddled after him, whining for him to wait up.

"Sweetie, if there's reincarnation, the next time I come back I'm going to have a glamorous career and pass on the children!" Sarah said.

Alex laughed, turned Sarah toward the door and gave her a gentle shove. "Go. Get your errands done, and have a double mocha at the espresso bar in the mall before you come back. Everything'll look better when you're full of caffeine."

"Thanks, Alex, I owe you," Sarah said, sailing out the door. She gave a jaunty wave as she crossed the lawn, calling over her shoulder, "Just don't try to claim later I didn't warn you!"

Alex quickly discovered what she meant. Lizabeth, who normally never shed a tear, threw a screaming fit when she discovered her mother was gone and then clung fussily to Alex's every move, while Brandon, who could generally be counted on to entertain himself, dogged her every footstep and came on like the Grand Inquisitor.

"What are you doing?" he asked, following her up the stairs as she clutched Lizabeth in one arm and Travis's clean laundry in the other. Entering her bedroom, she set the baby down on the floor and stacked the clothes on her bed. "I'm getting things ready to pack."

"Oh. Are you going on a trip? Daddy went to Sandman Crisco, you know."

She couldn't suppress a smile. "That's San Francisco, Bran."

"Right. So where are you going?"

"I'm not going anywhere," she said patiently. "Travis is. Remember?"

"But why can't he stay for our game tomorrow?"

She struggled to keep her voice matter-of-fact. "He just can't. He has to go back to Connecticut."

"But why?"

"Because that's where he lives." She racked her brain for something to distract him. "Didn't he tell you he has a horse and a cow and some goats?" She made a helpless gesture with her hand. "He needs to go home and see them."

"Do they miss him? Why can't they come here? Is he going to bring them back with him?"

So much for distractions. "Brandon, sweetie, Travis isn't coming back."

"Why?"

"Because this isn't his home. He lives in Connecticut. With the goats."

"Don't you want him to live with you anymore, Auntie Alex?"

"Of course I do, Brandon, but sometimes even grown-ups don't get to have things the way they want."

"Why not?"

"Because they have responsibilities, like a home and a job and a family. They have to think of those things first."

"I don't understand," he said predictably. "I thought Travis was your family now." His little face scrunched up in a perplexed frown. With the unintentional cruelty of children, he added, "You don't have anybody else."

"No, I don't," Alex agreed, leading him out of the bedroom and pulling the door partially closed, since Lizabeth had blessedly fallen asleep on the rug.

"Grown-ups are so stupid sometimes," Brandon remarked, hot on her heels as she crossed the hall to the stairwell closet.

"Yes, sometimes they are." Alex opened the closet door and turned on the inside light, then stood on the box she kept there so she could reach the rope to pull down the retractable metal ladder.

"Wow, rad," Brandon said, his eyes widening with curiosity. "What's that?"

"The ladder that goes to the attic." She pushed the hair from her eyes and climbed the first few rungs.

"Gee, neat!" Brandon was right behind her, his warm breath striking the back of her knees.

"Brandon, get down. This'll just take me a sec."

"But I want to see."

"Brandon."

"Please, Auntie Alex?"

She tried a different tack. "I need you to listen for Lizabeth," she explained. "How about if you come over next week when it's just you and me? We can explore."

Immediately, his voice brightened. "Really?"

"I promise."

"All *right!*" he said with little-boy glee. "Wait until I tell Sean. You won't let him come too, will you? You won't let Sean come, huh, Auntie Alex?" Brandon's persistent voice floated up from below. "Promise?"

"I *promise.*" It took a few minutes to find the suitcase she wanted, but once she did she lost no time making her way down the ladder, dragging it in her wake. By the time she set the case down in the hall, she could hear Lizabeth's disgruntled crying coming from the bedroom. "Oh, for cripes' sake." She snapped off the closet light.

"What do you want that old thing for?" Brandon asked, drawing pictures in the dust that had collected on the stiff sides of the suitcase.

"For Travis to put his clothes in," she explained. "But first we have to take it downstairs and clean it up."

"I can do that. Mommy says I'm really strong. I do lots of things for her." Trying to lift the bulky case, he staggered back under its weight.

She smiled as he grunted with effort. "I bet you do, kiddo, but this is filled with my brother's old fishing gear and it's too heavy for you." She took the case from him and set it at the head of the stairs, then went back to the closet to secure the ladder.

"But—" The shrilling of the telephone cut him off.

"Good grief." Alex swiped impatiently at a hank of hair that had fallen in her face. "Would you get that?" She nodded toward the room Travis had occupied when he was sick.

"Sure!" He raced down the hall. In a moment he yelled at the top of his lungs, "It's for Travis. Do you want me to tell 'em he isn't here?"

Shutting the closet door, she hurried toward the guest room, thinking dryly that whoever it was had probably already heard. "I'll tell them," she said to the child, taking the receiver from his hand. "Hello?"

"Cross not back yet?" came a gravely male voice.

"No, I'm sorry, he isn't in. Can I take a message?"

The caller gave a low chuckle. "You must be his friend." The twist he put on "friend" was suggestive but not objectionably so. "Well, honey, this is his boss, Derwin Mac-Gregor. We're getting ready to fly out of here, but I wanted to tell him again he did a damn good job. LeClair's still whining about that fantasy the boyo fed him about being retired and wanting a cut for returning the diamonds, but his lackeys are starting to sing like nightingales.

"So tell Cross he played it just right—and thank you for taking such good care of him, honey. Apparently LeClair had half the slime in Seattle searching for Cross, but it never occurred to him to check the 'burbs, thank God. Lucky for us some people are basically stupid, huh?" He paused, as if listening to something or somebody she couldn't hear, then said, "They're calling the flight. Tell the boyo I'll expect to see him in D.C. Monday morning at the latest. I've got a great assignment for him, in Greece. Oh, and let him know that we found the leak." His voice turned grim. "Tell him it *was* Stella—I'll explain later. Gotta go." And with that, he hung up.

Her knuckles white from the stranglehold she had on the receiver, Alex sank onto the edge of the bed since her knees were suddenly too weak to hold her, only vaguely aware that Lizabeth's cries had escalated into screams demanding her attention.

Yet she didn't move. She couldn't. She felt battered. Beaten. Betrayed. Key words and phrases ran through her mind.

A damn good job. Fantasy. He played it just right. Half the slime in Seattle searching for him. Basically stupid.

That last seemed tailor-made for her.

Had it all been a lie? Just part of his job? Had she simply provided a convenient port in the storm, a safe place to hide out, a little diversion from his job?

He'd never promised her anything, she reminded herself. He'd never said he cared, or told her any of those kinds of lies, and she knew Travis well enough to know he'd never do anything to put her in danger.

At least, she *thought* she knew Travis.

Now, she wasn't certain she knew anything.

"Auntie Alex?" Belatedly, she became aware that Brandon was clutching her hand, his face creased with worry. "Auntie Alex, Lizabeth's sure getting loud. Aren't you going to go get her?"

The concern in his voice snapped her out of her paralysis. Patting his hand, she took a deep breath and stood. "I guess I'd better, hadn't I?" Still slightly shaky, she started for the other room. "Aren't you coming?" she asked when Brandon remained standing by the bed.

He wrinkled his nose. "Nah. I hate it when Liza cries. It hurts my earbums."

Alex gave him a weak smile. "That's eardrums, Bran," she said, crossing the hall and going into the other room to soothe the overwrought toddler.

She'd barely gotten Liza calmed down when a loud thump jerked her attention toward the door. It was followed almost immediately by a strangled, terrified yelp, a series of heart-stopping thuds and then an awful, overwhelming silence.

With a terrible sense of foreboding, Alex clutched Lizabeth tight. Then, feeling as if a giant hand was closing around her throat, she raced to the top of the staircase and looked down.

It was a nightmare come to life.

Lying motionless on the lower landing was Brandon, the heavy suitcase half on top of him. He was totally still, showing not the faintest sign of life, and as Alex stared, she began to hear a terrible roaring in her hears. She swayed, nearly losing her balance as everything around her seemed to telescope, and she was afraid she was going to be sick.

By an act of will, she forced the faintness away, but it wasn't until Lizabeth pointed at Brandon and began to whimper that she found the strength to move. She flew down the stairs.

Still clutching the toddler, she lifted the heavy case away from Brandon's body, tossing it as if it weighed no more than a feather. Then she dropped to her knees, setting Liza behind her.

Although she couldn't see anything wrong, Brandon didn't move so much as an eyelash, and her panic grew. Hands shaking, she placed one against his throat to measure his pulse, and with the other gently began to probe for a lump or bump that might explain his unconsciousness.

Two things occurred almost simultaneously. The first was that, as she ran her fingers behind his left ear and around the back of his head, she encountered something warm and sticky. When she pulled her hand away, it was covered with glistening blood. And it was then, as she stared in horror at her scarlet fingers, her dripping palm, that she realized she couldn't find Brandon's pulse.

The room spun. She felt hot, and then so cold she began to shiver. She couldn't seem to catch her breath. She couldn't think. She didn't want to.

The entire scene was hauntingly familiar. She looked down with glazed eyes at the still, lifeless body sprawled at her feet, but she didn't see Brandon anymore.

It was Stefan lying there. Stefan, blond and handsome and laughing one moment, and in the next ... In the next, he'd been lying lifeless on the convenience-store floor, dead from the shotgun blast he'd taken in the neck at pointblank range, his warm red blood splattered across his new wife's horrified face.

Jamming her fist into her mouth to stifle a scream, Alex began to whimper. Then she snatched up Lizabeth, wrenched at the doorknob and bolted blindly out the front door.

* * *

Travis found her hours later at the hospital.

She sat in a low, molded chair in the emergency waiting room and watched as he walked toward her, the strong planes of his face standing out in sharp relief in the muted light of the inner corridor, his long legs eating up the distance between them as he moved with his usual lithe grace.

She sat frozen in an agony of indecision, the urge to fling herself at him tempered by an equally strong desire to rail at him.

I love you, Travis. The feeling poured from her heart.

Some people are basically stupid. His duplicity echoed through her mind.

Before she could do anything, he rocked to a stop before her and pulled her out of the chair and into his arms. "Thank God," he murmured into her hair, his heated whisper filled with the emotion that had been absent on his face. "When I got home and Connie told me you were at the hospital, it scared the hell out of me."

For just a moment, Alex savored the unthinking way he'd referred to her house as home and allowed herself the luxury of forgetting about the phone call. She leaned against him, letting the strength of his body support her, the heat of his skin warm her, the steady beat of his heart soothe her. It wasn't until a long moment later that she pressed her hands against the hard wall of his chest and tried to take a step away. It was impossible; his arms around her waist were as immovable as granite. "Didn't she tell you it was Brandon who was hurt?"

He looked down at her and despite a thorough search, she could see nothing but sincerity in his eyes as he admitted sheepishly, "I didn't stick around long enough to find out." One lean finger stroked her cheek and his voice dropped a notch. "I saw Sarah on my way in and she told me what happened."

Alex shivered involuntarily, remembering the events of the past few hours.

Seeing the slight but telltale motion, Travis gave her a quick, reassuring hug, his mind still grappling with Sarah's revelation regarding the manner of Stefan Zbresky's death. "Come on. Let's get you out of here," he said, ushering her toward the double-doored exit.

She balked, reluctant to leave in case she was still needed. "What about Brandon?"

"Brandon's going to be fine. The doctor says he probably won't even have to stay the night, and according to Sarah, Brad's on his way." He half-pushed, half-pulled her toward the Ferrari illegally parked in the driveway outside the entrance, and it wasn't until he went to ease her into the car that he registered her dishevelment. Her usually tidy hair looked like she'd spent the past hour in a wind tunnel, and her faded jeans and tattered sweatshirt were marked by rusty smears he realized must be Brandon's blood.

He went around and climbed behind the wheel, his voice gruff as he started the engine. "Don't worry about it. A dozen stitches and a mild concussion are little enough to show for that kind of tumble." He revved the engine and started out of the community hospital parking lot, headed for the freeway.

"I guess so," Alex said uncertainly, her mind and emotions reeling under the impact of the past few hours.

"I know so," he corrected gently. Her hesitancy was so unlike Alex's usual calm certainty it tore at his heart. He cleared his throat. "I'm proud of you. You didn't move Brandon, you called 911, you got Connie to watch Lizabeth and direct Sarah to the hospital. It must've been scary, but you did everything just right."

"For a while there, it was touch and go," Alex admitted with a faint, self-deprecating laugh. "I—I thought he was dead, and I was out the door and on the porch before I realized I was about to abandon him because of something that happened years ago."

"Yeah, but you didn't take off," he said, wondering at his own jumbled emotions. When Sarah had buttonholed him in the hallway, remarking in passing how well Alex had coped with Brandon's accident despite the trauma of Stefan's shooting, it had finally clicked in his mind. Suddenly, as vividly as if the details were there in front of him, he'd remembered the story of Stefan Zbresky's death and the gruesome picture some enterprising photographer had snapped directly after the shooting—pictures of Alex clutching her husband's shattered body to her breast. While a part of him felt nothing but compassion for what she'd gone through, another part of him felt angry as hell. Why hadn't she confided in him? Why hadn't she shared such an essential part of her history?

He remembered his words to her—and her reply. *You can hide away in your nice little suburb and pretend otherwise all you want, Alex, but the violence is still going on out there in the real world, believe me.*

Is that what you think, Travis? That I live a sheltered little life unaware of what goes on in your "real" world?

He winced, recalling his unintentional but no less patronizing tone, and something in his expression must have hinted at his thoughts.

"That must have been quite a little talk you and Sarah had," Alex said carefully, feeling an unexpected surge of resentment that she and her past had been discussed.

"Yeah, I guess it was." He glanced at her, noting her guarded expression. He shifted his eyes back to the road, and despite his best intentions, a hint of accusation crept into his voice. "Why didn't you tell me?"

"Tell you what?"

"About Stefan?" he said flatly.

She stiffened. "He died. Isn't that enough?" Hearing the slight quiver in her voice, she tried hard to put a brake on her emotions, but it was too late. The control she'd so hastily patched together following Brandon's fall began to disintegrate.

Travis was too caught up trying to repair his own crumbling composure to notice. Although his voice remained low, it held an almost savage undertone. "No, by God, it isn't!" Normally a conservative driver at best, it was a measure of his agitation that as they left the freeway and took the road leading east to Alex's, the speedometer was at sixty-five and climbing. "You let me believe he'd been the victim of an accident, not that some hopped-up kid with a gun shot him during a robbery."

Every word was a hammer blow chipping away at Alex's control. "Stefan's dead," she said around the growing lump in her throat, fighting against an urge to shout at him to leave her alone. She stared fixedly at the scenery whipping by. "What do you want? Do you want to hear about how on the fourth day of my honeymoon I saw my husband literally get his head blown off? Do you want details, Travis? Do you need to know that the force of the blast knocked him into my arms? That he was dead before I could even say goodbye? That I was covered in his blood and that I had nightmares about it for weeks, for months, for years? It's *over*. Let it go, Travis."

But he couldn't. Just the thought of what she'd been through made him half-crazy. "Stop it, Alex," he said fiercely, giving the wheel of the car a vicious wrench that sent it fishtailing into her driveway. He slammed on the brakes. "I wasn't asking for those kind of details and you know it! I just think you might have told me the truth."

"Truth?" It was the one word coming from him guaranteed to set her off. She unsnapped her seat belt and swiveled to face him. "If you want to discuss the truth, *Agent* Cross, let's start with you. A man named MacGregor called here earlier today looking for you. He said to tell you you'd done a good job with LeClair and that he's arranged your next assignment—I believe he mentioned Greece. Oh, and he said something about people being basically stupid. I assume he was referring to criminals, but then again, maybe he was talking about me!" She wrenched open the car door and got out, the effort she was making to restrain herself apparent in the careful way she closed the door.

Travis got out, as well, but with none of her restraint. He nearly ripped the door from its hinges when he opened it and then rocked the entire vehicle down to its tires when slamming it shut. "Don't call yourself stupid!" he shouted as they squared off across the Ferrari's top.

And just like that, her control was gone. "Why not?" she shouted back. "I swallowed every lie you told me, didn't I?"

"I didn't lie to you," he retorted furiously, even as the guilt at his deception washed through him. "I just didn't tell you everything! I was on assignment—what was I supposed to say? Excuse me, can I use your phone? I hope you don't mind, but I have a prior commitment to play mind games on the bastard responsible for my best friend's death? I can just imagine what you would have said to that!"

"Well, pardon me, but you must have contracted creative amnesia along with the chicken pox! Or did I dream it when you told me you were 'in the process' of retiring? That it 'takes a little time'?"

He slammed his open palm down on the car top. "So okay! I let you believe what you wanted to believe. It was easier that way—"

"Easier for whom?" she interrupted shrilly. "For me, Travis? Or for you? I trusted you. I never would've let myself fall in love with you if I'd known you were active in your job!" Even as she said the words, Alex knew it was a lie—nothing could have stopped her from loving him. Yet the past few hours had taken their toll; every time she closed her eyes she saw first Stefan and then Brandon lying still as death itself; it took no great imagination to see Travis lying there, as well. "I already lost one husband to some loony with a gun! I couldn't stand to lose another one!"

"So who's asking you to?" he roared, only to be rocked by a wave of remorse as tears started to spill down her cheeks.

Damn it all, anyway! It was all his fault. He'd reduced her to this; he taken her nice, ordered world and torn it to pieces. A picture flashed in his mind of Alex the first night they'd met, of her unruffled calm, of her serenity, and he ran a hand through his already rumpled hair, muttering a virulent oath as he contrasted that image to the pale, anguished woman before him.

Pain knifed through him, lines of tension bracketing his mouth. "I'm all wrong for you, Alex," he said, trying to make her see what he'd known all along. "You deserve someone who still believes in dreams, in the future. I left that behind years ago."

Her voice was thick with misery. "That's the biggest lie of all, Travis, and the sad thing is, you believe it. Oh, I don't doubt it's partly true, but that's only one facet of who you are. You're also the man who took the time to teach Brandon how to hit a ball, the man who created Milton Monster, a creature who counsels little boys in hope and patience and the idea that eventually the good guy takes the day. You made me feel like a woman again. What about that part of you, Travis?''

More than anything in the world he wanted to believe her, but the long, empty years alone had not been without cost—and as he watched, she looked down at her bloodstained clothing and shuddered, confirming what he'd known all along. He wasn't the right man for her. She was sunshine and flowers and dreams; he was unrelenting rain on a cold, dismal day—and tears. Why, why wouldn't she see it?

Frustrated by her refusal to face facts and hurting from the very truths she had to be made to see, he lashed out. ''So what are you saying here, Alex? Are you saying you want me but not my job? Well, I've got news for you, lady—it's a package deal. If you want me, you get the job, too, and I can't promise I won't come home in a body bag one day.''

His deliberate cruelty made its mark as the last of the color drained from her already pasty face. Involuntarily she took a step back. ''Please,'' she said on an agonized whisper. ''I can't.''

''Then don't talk to me about love, lady,'' he said coldly. ''I don't need what you're offering. I'll do just fine on my own.''

At his words, the gentle glow that had always illuminated Alex disappeared, and Travis felt as if his guts were being ripped out. With a few words, he'd managed to accomplish what even her husband's death hadn't done. He'd robbed her of her hope. *It had to be done,* he told himself. But that was scant comfort as he saw the blank expression in her eyes.

''Alex…'' Did he really say her name, or did he only think it? Without even realizing what he was doing, he started to reach out to her, but she was already turning away.

"I'm sorry," she said brokenly, raising a hand to dash away the tears tracking down her face and then automatically wiping it on her jeans—across the largest of the bloodstains. She glanced at the specks of blood on her hand—and then her face crumpled and she was gone, running down the walkway, the screen door slapping shut behind her as she fled into the house.

Powerless to stop her flight, Travis whirled, slamming his fist into the carport support, the pain in his hand nothing compared to the agony in his heart. *Well, hell.* What had he expected? Hadn't he known right from the start that he was no damn good for her, that she didn't deserve the kind of worry and turmoil he'd bring into her life? Hadn't he known he'd be courting disaster if he broke his rule about getting involved?

Hadn't he told Alex he wasn't cut out for happily-ever-after?

So who cared? He'd survived the past thirty or so years alone—he imagined he could match it with another thirty. He didn't need this—not any of it. Not the warm, welcoming house, not the slightly offbeat neighbors, not the kid next door with the innovative vocabulary—and sure as hell not the warm, beautiful blonde who drove like a maniac and made love like an angel.

Telling himself over and over he was doing the right thing, he threw himself into the Ferrari, revved the engine and slammed the stick into reverse, sending the sleek black car shooting out of the driveway. Yet even as he shifted into first and drove away, he felt a vast, aching emptiness inside and knew it was because he was leaving his heart behind.

Twelve

Duffel bag over his shoulder, Travis locked the front door of his Connecticut house and walked into the yard where his ancient pickup stood. More out of habit than any great fondness, he stopped to take one last look through his dark glasses at his modest little farm.

In the weeks he'd been gone, first to Seattle and from there to Greece, nothing had changed. Although everything was neat and tidy, the barn still needed a new roof, several fences were in need of repair, and the house was in desperate need of a fresh coat of pain.

Well, it was somebody else's headache now, he thought without a single pang of regret. A plaintive bleating interrupted his perusal, and with a sigh he walked over to a large wire mesh pen to say goodbye to Bonzo. He leaned down to scratch the small, black goat's head—and before he could snatch back his hand Bonzo bit him.

Behind his glasses, Travis's eyes narrowed. "You better clean up your act, pal," he told his diminutive attacker conversationally. "Up until this morning, Jack was just someone I paid to take care of you. But now that he's the new owner, he may not be as understanding of your little escapades. He might make you into a bota bag." Bonzo grinned at him and made a sound that sounded suspiciously like a laugh, then turned and walked away with an irreverent wag of his stubby tail.

Travis looked ruefully at the faint teeth marks that showed up white against the teak-colored skin on the back of his hand and shook his head. It wasn't surprising he was tanned. It had been hot in Athens. Hot, dull and frustrating. He'd had lots of time to think. And he hadn't been there a day before he'd known he'd made a major mistake.

He'd finally remembered something about his job he'd forgotten in the trauma of the past few months: he was sick of it. Tired to the depths of his soul. Even before Joel had been killed, he'd been disheartened by the ugliness of his everyday world. He'd been disenchanted with the hopelessness and sad endings, and somewhere deep inside, a little kernel of longing for an occasional moment of happiness had taken root, demanding a chance to thrive.

So he'd created *The Great Beyond* as a compromise. As Alex had so perceptively seen, it had become his refuge, a place to preserve what was left of his hopes and dreams, a buffer against his loneliness. And when the book had been accepted for publication, he'd actually begun to dream of leaving the State Department for good.

Then Joel had been murdered, and he'd become so consumed by the need for revenge that everything else had ceased to matter—until Alex had rescued him, miraculously scaling all the walls he'd thrown up, serenely refusing to see what a lost cause he was, willing to forgive him anything, even at the last, when she'd discovered how he'd lied to her and abused her trust.

He'd panicked, pure and simple. And not because he was afraid he couldn't be the man Alex thought he was, or the man he felt she deserved; when he was with her, he *was* that man. No, as much as he hated to admit it, he'd been afraid she'd leave him like his dad and his mom and Joel.

Travis felt the familiar tightening in his gut. There wasn't an hour of a day of the past few weeks that he hadn't thought about that last encounter with Alex. He'd driven to the airport like a man possessed, stopped barely long enough to arrange the return of her car with the resident agent, then used the money Mac had advanced him for a ticket on the next flight to Washington, D.C. Stubbornness and sheer momentum had carried him through the next twenty-four hours. Once in the capital, he'd gone straight to the office to pick up his passport, said a few choice words to Tinny Voice and stoically ignored the knowing look in Mac's eyes when the older man briefed him. In no time at all he'd been enjoying the dubious benefits of the heat in southern Greece, trying to protect a crass young consulate official who seemed determined to get them both killed by carrying on a torrid love affair with another official's wife.

And all the while, like a VCR gone berserk, his mind had continuously replayed the cruel way he'd broken Alex's heart and forfeited her trust before he'd even had the courage to tell her what she meant to him. Because somewhere between chicken pox and chicken soup, between "pubatory" and "accelerations," he'd fallen in love—only to foolishly throw it away.

But hearts can be mended, he reminded himself. Hearts can be mended and trust can be regained—Alex had taught him that, and it was the only thing he'd found comfort in during the weeks they'd been apart.

He took one last, long look around the place that had never been his home and then walked briskly back to the truck and climbed inside. And without a single backward glance, he closed the door on his past and drove away.

The problem with men, Alex thought darkly, as the Ferrari sputtered to a stop in the driveway while an old Carpenters' tune about love gone wrong wafted from the tape deck, *is their total unpredictability.* One little tiff and there was no telling what crazy thing they might do—like steal your car and leave the country.

She bit her lip at the crushing sense of remorse that rolled through her as she thought about what she'd said to Travis to inspire such behavior. Clicking off the engine, she set the parking brake and then leaned listlessly back against the soft leather upholstery, trying to summon up the energy to get out of the car and carry the small, single shopping bag holding her frozen dinner into the house. Instead, the internal dialogue she'd been having off and on ever since she'd realized Travis was really gone began again. *Great job,* said the little voice in her head.

"Don't start," she told herself sternly. She didn't want to indulge in self-recriminations anymore; what she wanted, more than life itself, was a chance to explain. She needed to tell Travis how she'd reverted that day to the person she'd been before he came into her life, to the woman who'd been afraid to risk anything for fear of losing everything.

He needed to know she wasn't that woman anymore. He deserved to know that it was loving him that had changed her. She was finished with hiding from life—and ready to fight for a chance to share it with him. If only she could see him again to tell him.

But as far as she knew, he was still out of the country. Lord knew, she'd single-handedly worn out the State Department phone system trying to locate him. After three weeks, she and the switchboard operator, a very nice woman named Laverne, were on a first-name basis, and Laverne had promised to call if there was any news of his return.

So far, Alex had heard nothing.

Lethargically picking up the bag, Alex finally got out of the car and started toward the back porch, the sense of desolation that was her constant companion these days weighing her footsteps. Caught up in memories, she headed for the stoop, paying no attention to her surroundings until an unfamiliar fragrance teased her nose. Her steps slowed and her head came up and she tried to identify the foreign sweetness.

She stared in wonder.

There were flowers everywhere. Roses in white and red and pink; petunias and alyssum, geraniums, marigolds, impatiens and a dozen other varieties she couldn't put a name to. They were in clay pots and plastic tubs, in baskets hanging from the eaves, in a trio of antique washtubs and a painted apple crate. There was even something with feathery leaves and little blue blowers planted in one of her old tennis shoes.

Travis. Even as she told herself to get serious, her heart began to pound in her chest. But who else could it be? Sarah maybe—or Brandon? But no—even they would never go this far to cheer her up.

Travis. Just imagining him here was too much to hope for.

Her heart in her mouth, she forced herself to move, walking slowly toward the stairs—and then she saw him standing there, hidden in the deep shadows of the porch, as big and dark and handsome as he was every night when he came to her in her dreams.

His expression guarded by a pair of dark glasses, he moved into the sunlight and looked down at her, his voice strangely rusty as he said softly, "Hello, Alex."

Her pulse rate rocketed toward the sky while her stomach dropped through the floor. Clutching the grocery bag, she drank in the sight of him. "Travis." His presence was so longed for—and yet so unexpected—she didn't know what to say. She gestured at the bank of flowers. "Did you do this?"

Moving slowly, almost as if he was afraid any sudden movement would make her bolt, he came down the steps and took the bag out of her hands. "Yeah."

"But why?"

Wrapping a big, warm hand around her elbow, he guided her onto the porch and said hoarsely, "I never gave you flowers before."

"Oh," she said inanely, still unable to think of an intelligent thing to say. He looks tired, she thought, feeling as if a giant hand were squeezing her heart. His clothes were rumpled, his thick, dark hair desperately in need of a cut, and there were new lines scored between his nose and his mouth.

"Alex," he said quietly. "We need to talk."

This was not at all the way she'd envisioned things going when she saw him again. She'd planned what she needed to say—and she'd planned on leading up to it much more subtly. But there was such an air of detachment about him she couldn't put it off a second longer. "I was wrong," she blurted out.

"Wrong?" he echoed, a foreign note of alarm in that oddly husky voice.

"That day. In the driveway. I was tired and upset and afraid, and I forgot something. Something important."

"Yeah?" he rasped. "And what was that?"

"I forgot that the one thing worse than losing you—" it was an effort to get the words out around the growing lump in her throat "—would be never having the opportunity to show you how much I love you. I love you, Travis, and I don't care what you are—writer or artist or agent." Afraid to hope, unable not to, she waited for his reaction.

It was not at all what she expected. He reached up and pulled his sunglasses off, his hand hovering for a moment to rub the bridge of his nose. Finally, after what seemed like a long, long time, he turned and looked down at her. "How do you feel about unemployed? I quit my job this morning."

Their gazes met and held, Alex's heart turning over as she saw that his navy eyes were bright with unshed tears. Seeing the hope and naked longing on his face, she suddenly understood the significance of his raspy voice. "Oh, Travis," she cried. And with that she launched herself across the narrow distance between them and into his arms.

He reeled her in with the desperation of a dying man receiving a second chance. "I went to my place," he choked out. "But without you it wasn't home, so I sold it to my neighbor." He pulled her closer. "I didn't leave that day because of what you said about my job—I left because I was afraid. I tried to tell myself I was doing it for you, but that was just a part of it. The truth was, with my track record..." He shrugged and let the sentence die, then cleared his throat and began anew, "Everyone I ever loved left me— I was afraid to even try. But I love you, Alex. And if you'll still have me, I want to give us a chance." His arms closed around her like he'd never let her go, and then his mouth found hers for a slow, tender kiss.

Alex kissed him back with everything she possessed, her own eyes damp with tears. When they finally came up for air she leaned weakly against the warm wall of his chest and said quietly, but with all seriousness, "I'm not ever letting you go. Understand?"

A guy would have to be a fool to argue with that. "I hope not," Travis said, savoring the feel of her in his arms. His face infused with tenderness, he reluctantly pushed her away because he wanted—he needed—to see her face. He brushed his thumb across her chin. "I want it all, Alex. Marry me?"

"Are you sure?" she asked very, very softly. The joy lighting her features was breathtaking.

"Absolutely." He gave her a slow, sexy smile, then leaned down and pressed a series of kisses along the line of her jaw before confiding in a husky whisper, "I have it on the best authority," he confided, nuzzling the sensitive skin behind her ear, "that any man who married you would get an angel in his life and a bobfire in his bed."

"Well, in that case—" she twined her arms around his neck and began to kiss him back "—I guess the answer has to be yes."

And as their lips searched and finally met, an exuberant victory yell came from the direction of Sarah's house, followed by Brandon's joyful cry of "All-l-l right!"

Alex and Travis were too busy to notice.

Epilogue

Ensconced in the sleek black Ferrari, Travis and Alex raced through the warm summer night. Even as the speedometer edged past the legal limit, Travis continued to accelerate, his blue eyes dark with anxiety as he negotiated the sparse Saturday night traffic. Sparing a quick glance at his very pregnant wife's pale face, he said, "I told you we shouldn't have stayed for that last inning."

"But it was the championship game, Travis. You had to be there. The Sluggers needed you." Even as another contraction began—they were coming now with alarming regularity—her voice remained calm. "I can't believe they actually won," she went on. "The look on Brandon's face when he hit that homer was price...less." Despite Alex's determination not to alarm her husband of two years, she had to grip the dash to keep from crying out as the labor pain peaked, and the last word she uttered was little more than a sibilant hiss.

She took a deep breath and told herself sternly she did *not* feel a need to push. Instead, between a series of ragged little pants, she thought about the night their baby was conceived, the very night that Travis had won the prestigious children's literary award for his second Milton Monster book, *Beyond the Great Beyond*.

"Alex?" Travis questioned as they pulled up to the emergency room entrance and the Ferrari jerked to a stop.

"Travis, I think we're going to have the baby. *Now.*"

"*Well, hell!*" He gave the horn an ear-shattering blast before leaping out of the car and racing around to pull open her door. With infinite care he swept her up into his arms and started for the hospital doors.

"I love you, Travis," Alex said softly.

He rocked to a halt. "Oh, lady. I love you, too." He pressed a quick but achingly tender kiss to her soft lips. "So very, very much." Then he straightened, pushed his way through the swinging doors, strode into the brightly lit hospital—and proceeded to bellow for help.

A very short time later, Joel Alexander Cross was born.

* * * * *

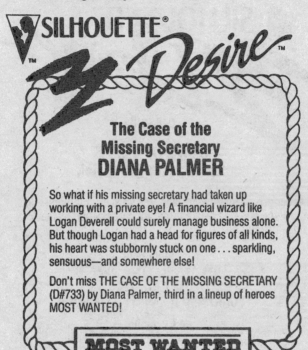